Those Who Had Known Love

Those Who Had Known Love

(Jara Bhalobesechhilo)

Anita Agnihotri

Translated from the Bengali by
Rani Ray

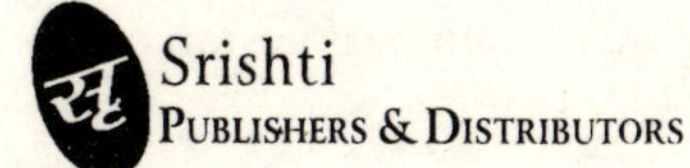
Srishti
Publishers & Distributors

Srishti Publishers & Distributors
64-A, Adhchini
Sri Aurobindo Marg
New Delhi 110017

Published by Srishti Publishers & Distributors 2000

The translator gratefully acknowledges the advice and guidance given by the author in her translation of the novel *Jara Bhalobesechhilo*. She would also like to thank Sonali Prakash for her careful reading and valuable assistance in editing the work.

ISBN 81-87075-56-2
Rs. 145.00

Cover Paintings by Samir Das
Cover Design by Arrt Creations
45 Nehru Apartment, New Delhi 110019
e-mail: arrt@vsnl.com

Printed and bound in India by
Saurabh Print-O-Pack, Noida

Contents

Biographical Notes

Born in 1956 in Calcutta, Anita Agnihotri (née Chattopadhyay) started writing poetry in her early childhood. Her poems were published by Satyajit Ray in his monthly *Sandesh* in 1969. Married to Satish Agnihotri from Maharastra in 1982 and with two children, Anita Agnihotri is now fully into several areas of creative activity which include poetry, short stories, novels, childrens literature, essays and water colour painting. As a member of Indian Administrative Service, she has travelled widely all over the country and has worked in Bihar, Orissa and West Bengal. Her stories essentially focus on common people's struggles and aspirations and their immense faith in fellow human beings. She has three volumes of short stories, two novels, four volumes of children's stories and several volumes of poetry to her credit. *Those Who Had Known Love* is the English translation of her second novel, *Jara Bhalobesechhilo*.

Rani Ray read English at Bedford College, London and University of California from where she obtained her PhD degree. She has taught English Literature at the Universities of Delhi and California. She has translated Suchitra Bhattacharya's novel *Bhangan Kaal* (*Falling Apart*) and has co-translated two anthologies of contemporary Bangla short stories.

Author's Preface

Those Who Had Known Love (Jara Bhalobesechhilo) is my second novel. It was originally published by Mitra O Ghosh, a leading publisher of Bengali fiction and essays, in 1998. The novel was not serialised or published in any periodical before it was brought out as a book. This is rather unusual for a young Bengali writer. My perennial problem is my lack of ability or inclination to accommodate a long narrative in the tight space provided by a periodical or time it in tune with the demands of a festive season when 'special' issues are published. I recall that I had taken the whole manuscript, weighing nearly a kilogram, to Sabitendranath Roy of Mitra O Ghosh who after reading the manuscript, in frank indulgence to a young writer, okayed its publication for the Calcutta Book Fair, 1998.

To me, Mitra O Ghosh is very special because they are an institution in themselves, reflected in their continuous interaction with Bengal's literary heritage. Also, they are publishers of Bibhuti Bhushan Bandopadhyay – a writer whom two generations of Bengali readers simply adore. The two old rooms in the ground floor of 10 Shyama Charan Dey Street, Calcutta, with walls on both sides stacked with books, had seen the literary giants of Bengal – Bibhuti Bhusan, Tarashankar, Gajendra Mitra, Saiyad Mujtaba Ali, Promotha Nath Bishi – sitting and chatting over tea and *moori-chanachoor*.

Even now, I feel a tremendous sense of elation and inspiration when I go to Mitra O Ghosh and am extremely proud that I have been included in their list of authors. I must add that my collection of short stories, *Chandan Rekha*, was published by them in 1997.

The novel was slowly growing within me for about a decade. But I wrote *Mahuldihar Din (The Days of Mahuldia)* first, in 1994, propelled by a feeling of isolation and nostalgia for home during my stay in England. *Mahuldihar Din* should ideally have been a sequel to *Jara Bhalobesechhilo*. My homecoming to Calcutta in 1996 brought back to my mind the memories of the city during the seventies: a place that had changed forever. Calcutta during the peak of the naxalite movement – of sleepless nights, police patrols, raids and arrests, retained a core: a very romantic, idealistic core, where love and sacrifice made for love were considered glorious. Young boys and girls of the city were very different from their likes in the nineties. Big money, big Capital and dreams of prosperous life abroad had not mesmerised them so immensely. Calcutta was not a globalised metropolis then and her quiet winter afternoons had a charming glow of an old landscape painting. Melodies of Rabindra Sangeet would overflow the bylanes and reach the noisy main roads, and the late evening radio broadcasts carried the unmistakable strain of western classical music.

Rukmini and Phalgun represent this Calcutta of the seventies. They had grown up together like twin saplings and had shared a happy and creative childhood and adolescence. Professional career takes Ruku away from the city and far away into the cloudy terrains of Mussoorie where she comes across the melting cauldron of the vast, complex India – so many young people like her, from different corners of the country, questing for India, that is, Bharat: Navroj and Kuldeep, Sunila and Swarup and many others like them. All are fresh and young and trying to cope with the new realities of life. The story moves from Mussoorie to Madhaya Pradesh, from Bihar to Calcutta and back, in its own rythm. All the characters are fictitious. People have got fused and recreated in my mind, and different entities from those whom I had actually seen and encountered have emerged. But *the* India is very real, the abysmal poverty is real, so are the darkness and the processes of development against the backdrop of silence of the majority. The narrative also unfolds the initial impact of these hard realities on the young people – where is the real India? Can the 'State', as people see it, be moulded? What is development – without the mobilisation of people?

In the end, after fire engulfs the Mussorrie campus, it is again Phalgun the young lover, who emerges victorious: love enables him to recreate his lost symphony.

The narrative has captured a lot of my own self though it is not autobiographical. It captures the way I look at life, the country and its people. It celebrates the sense of bonding I feel with the world in general and with nature in particular; it shows what keeps me going as a writer.

I am more thrilled by the fact, Rani Ray, who has read widely different kinds of literature, has translated the novel. 'Srishti' has taken upon itself the task of reaching the book to readers who may not to able to read it in the original. I remain indebted to them.

Anita Agnihotri

Alipur

Calcutta, January, 2000

One

The ground was not exactly circular but oval, shaped like an egg, constructed with skill from stones and earth dredged up from the highlands and enclosed by a concrete wall on all sides. A concrete footway, bounded by railings, coiled all the way up. The lecture hall was situated high above, as also an office and a dispensary. Men's hostels stood in various places a couple of slopes below. Further down were tennis-courts, areas marked out for badminton and volleyball. There were so many hollows, descents and gentle valleys nestling on the bosom of the mountains. Houses like in picture post-cards, gardens, big halls were placed here and there. Raising her face upward from the riding-ground where she stood, Ruku could see the evening descending rapidly, spreading its wings. Today the sun had set without pausing to cavort in the light.

The sky was cloudy at the end of March. The air was chilly. One felt the cold even more when the body was wet with perspiration, after a stretch of riding. Rukmini lifted her light maroon coat, flung on rocks below the railings and flopped it on her shoulders. Further above, leftward, the floating clouds in the sky were slowly smudging a long line of pine trees, the small huts of the hillfolk as well. Here, from time to time without warning, clouds descend to the eye-level, then the scene in the front gets blotted out.

Clouds were moving down.

The heels of her new riding boots made a *tak tak* sound as Ruku rapidly climbed up the steep concrete road. Her khaki breeches were easy around the waist but uncomfortable above the knees: she found it difficult to double up her legs. Tailor Munilal had come to their Block and himself taken the measurements for the shirt and breeches. He said they would stretch after a few days wearing. The shirt fitted her perfectly, but she felt uncomfortable all the time. She was used to wearing sarees in Calcutta; here she took a *chunni* whenever she put on *salwar-kameez*. With simply a shirt on she felt self-conscious. No one stared back at her yet she thought all kinds of people, abandoning their work, were gaping at her.

A dark tarred road wound its way from where the steps ended, leaving the main Block behind. It reached the post office traversing the Director's bungalow and the green lawns. It slanted downwards from front of the post office, a small building with a wooden roof and a wooden veranda. There was an ancient telephone there: one had to wait for hours to get through to Calcutta after booking a call, and a wooden table sticky with glue. That's where Ruku placed her envelopes, wrote her home address, addresses of relatives and of one other person. There's an indescribable smell of the woods in the little post office, imparting the melancholy mood of a late afternoon singed by the dying sun. Ruku liked coming there.

She was not going out anywhere today but was returning early to her Block. There was a presentation tomorrow involving the four in her group. She must go over the lecture notes. The perspiration in her body had dried. She must take off those impossible clothes at once.

Shyamakanta Sinha was standing in the corner of the street. A man from Bihar, he was their Economics teacher; dark complexioned and very quiet. He had come to Mussoorie straight from the Planning Commission. Seeing him, Ruku took out her right hand from beneath her coat and saluted him with folded palms. She tried hard to wrap the jacket around herself, but there was little time for that. Sinha stroked her head with his index finger and grinned "Thinking what I'm doing standing in the evening in front of the Ladies Block, eh?"

"Not at all," Ruku turned red.

"See!" he raised his hand towards the branches of an ancient pine tree which almost touched the sky. "See, there ..." A flapping noise came from the dry branches and twigs. Something was going on – such clamour! A lot of withered pine cones and bits of snapped twigs lay strewn on the ground.

"A squirrel – about to scoot. I see its face every evening. It has just slipped in. Keep watching ..."

Two men appeared, laughing away, before the squirrel could escape. Kuldeep was wearing a purple turban, Navroj didn't have one on.

How unfortunate! Ruku quickly hid behind Shyamakanta Sinha. Today she had purposely held back at the riding ground till late. The stone steps, the paths, the neon-lit roads get riveted with laughter, chatter and peals of delight of small groups emerging from the riding ground, the tennis-court or the film club at five in the evening. Ruku had remained standing alone in the ground to avoid them. Kripal Singh, the trainer, had called out to her before he left. She heard him only after an interval, so absent-minded was she. The horses had trotted off on the wet grass, soundless in spite of their hooves. Their nut-brown, black and white bodies threw off a peculiar steam. A kind of sweaty smell was coming from their mane. Ruku breathed the upturned palm of her hand to see if some smell of horses hugged her body. She hadn't met anyone so far ... couldn't those two have made the scene a few minutes later?

Kuldeep smiled from ear to ear. He was amused seeing Ruku trying to make herself invisible.

"Sir, she's shy. She's riding for the first time, you see."

Shyamakanta Sinha turned around good humouredly, placing his hands in his pockets.

"What, feeling shy because of me ...? Why, to me she's a child. You two are the unexpected nuisance. Go, get lost."

"We are clearing out ..." Kuldeep pretended to scamper off.

Navroj didn't utter a word. He thrust a half-roasted corn-cob into Ruku's hands. "Bought it at the Library corner ... take a bite." Kuldeep looked back, walking some distance. His brown eyes were sparkling with delight. The sky had turned purple ... soon the distant scene would become hazy and vanish.

"Rukmini, Ma and Babuji arrived from Thiog this afternoon. Drop by at G B Pant Hostel after dinner."

Entering her room Ruku found Kusum lying, face buried in the pillow, her long golden hair sloped along her back. The bit of waist that peeped in-between the red silk saree and the red blouse was as white as ivory. She must have got dressed to go somewhere and now lay sulking. Ruku was extremely harassed by this moody obstinate girl. She longed to love her. Kusum was so beautiful, so perfect in every way, her nose, her eyes, brows as if painted by brush, a slightly cracked husky voice. Was she fragile because she was so beautiful? Her mood waxed and waned like the waves at sea. She laughed at one moment, sobbed the next, flared up in anger at other times. And there were always visitors for her waiting below. Some with the excuse of handing over lecture notes, others with casettes of songs, some came to invite her for a drama rehearsal. Lord knows why she was in such a temper!

Ruku took off her boots and socks and pushed them beneath the bed. She made her way to the bathrooom, taking her lounging gown along. The bathroom was next to the veranda at the back of the building, its wooden floor creaked as she walked. Water was kept boiling twenty-four hours a day in the huge wooden pitcher, by electricity. For a while she stood in the veranda, resting her hands on the railings. A huge moon was up that night, slightly eaten away in one corner. Yet light flooded the entire scene. The Himalayas, the Kumaon mountain range seemed plastered against the sky. The peaks of Badrinath, Banorpuchha hill range glowed in the winter afternoons – like some unsheathed sword piercing the dense blue. But ice had not as yet begun to melt on the mountain tops; below, the black rocks bared themselves a little. Dissolved snow ran to the rivers in the tableland lower down. In the dark of night you could hardly see anything. The icy fingers of the mountain breeze brushed against Rukmini's cheeks, her forehead, as if to proclaim they exist. "I come from the mountains," they declared. The flat-topped highland is covered with a dense yellow-green forest of all kinds of deciduous and evergreen trees. The dark green of the distant trees, the light-green and tawny colour of those close by become sharp as they catch daylight. Then one can see patches of grass growing close to the forest. A human pathway from where the grassland ends, bends and extends to some distance, making its way to the huts, shops, granaries belonging to those who live outside the campus. Now in the moonlight all appeared non-existent; hidden like the unspoken distress pervading domestic work. Ruku turned her gaze away from the profound evanascent beauty of the mighty sky and went in to wash her hands.

Kusum in bed, lying on her stomach meant there was trouble

in store for Ruku today. All would be well if she got up and went for dinner; if not, Ruku would have to go to the dining hall and ask for room-service, with her permission. It was far more likely she would say, "Don't bother, I won't eat – nothing will happen, go and have your dinner." In which case she would have to run to the lounge, seek out Raj or Gaurav and they would bring her icecream or chowmien at midnight, at their peril. This was a routine Ruku had got used to in the last six months along with little irritations: for example, Kusum going off to sleep before eight, and her having to carry on her studies by the table lamp. At times, on the very same night when Ruku was about to doze off with a heater on for the winter cold, a double blanket pulled up to her ears, Mehedi Hassan's ghazals would start blaring from the side table; the glass bangles around Kusum's arms would jangle and she would sing with a husky voice. Such a hassle!

Rukmini turned the pages of her lecture notes, half reclining on the bed. The notes on Political Science and Economics were intelligible enough. One could make sense of them in spite of the bad handwriting. But what a hotch-potch when it came to the Indian Constitution! The Ordinances were legible enough, but big gaps loomed where their implications ought to have been. For that no other than Professor Ramesh Sharma, who had an uncanny resemblance to Zulfikar Ali Bhutto, was responsible. That gentleman would jump up and run towards the students's gallery, the minute he began lecturing. The gallery had rows of chairs placed on each of its steps. He would scramble up the steps while talking, bounce down excitedly, countering his own arguments, one by one. All of them save those KT's i.e. the keen types, sitting in the two front rows would look at him, eyes wide in amazement: not a word would get written. Sharma would halt as if he had sniffed gun-powder smoke if a question were put to him. Looking fiercely, pucker his brows he would say, "Please, please (with an extra emphasis on the last syllable), don't misunderstand me ..."

"Please, please ..." mimicking him, Rukmini laughed, all by herself, rolling her head on the pillow. She gazed at the white ceiling for a few moments, then as she turned her face towards the table lamp noticed an unopened blue inland letter.

When did it arrive? She hadn't seen it before. The lamp swayed as she pulled at the edge of the blue paper. Kusum was up. She sat on the bed, opened a small box of *panmasala* and munching some she said, "Agamchand came and left it. It was lying in your locker."

"Shall I ask for room-service for you?" Ruku laughed.

"No, for God's sake! You are put to trouble everyday. Stay – I'll go myself." A phantom of red silk coasted to the rear balcony throwing a mild scent in the room.

Ruku held the letter next to her nose for sometime then opened it. The air of this country has a smell about it different from the special scent of mist and pine leaves. That smell had hit her when the jeep had speeded ahead, crossing a huge yellow arch making a loud groan. Suppose some of it lingered in the letter? Familiar handwriting and a well-known address! The blue paper didn't show any sign it had come from afar. But each time it arrived, to Ruku it seemed not-a-letter but Phalgun who faced her, travelling a long distance. In this way – Ma, Baba, Dida and friends came to her. Their colourful images became alive against the spotless blue of the letter on one day or another. Today she felt Phalgun had come.

"Dear me! studying so hard that you don't get the time to write! Have kept count – not a single letter from you in twenty-six days! You've passed your exams, where's the need now to study so much? Yesterday I went to Melody and bought you Beethoven's ninth symphony – be sure you don't go and listen to it elsewhere! Mashima is always so sad, every evening her eyes are full of tears ... hope you haven't stopped writing poetry. I'll hit you on the head on the day of *Ashtami* if you become too much of a bureaucrat!"

Phalgun – with a head full of unoiled curly hair, deep, dark-brown eyes, gaunt face, so fair complexioned that veins on the skin of his arms were visible – that Phalgun had written, "You must send me your new compositions – poetry. I'll send it to *Sandesh* ..."

The yellow gulmohar flowers lay scattered on the pavements of Harish Mukherjee Road, drifting along the street when there was a current of air – harsh sounds from machines, smell of wheat chaffs. The two of them had walked intruding into the evening's *azaan*. Phalgun marched in front, slinging a shoulder bag, Ruku behind him. Their shoulders touched when they came together.

"Ei Ruku, you must think of me at least once everyday ... as you stand against the iron railing next to the post office, from where you can see the contours of the mountains. I will wring your neck if you think of someone else ..."

Inside the Puja pandal, on *Ashtami* day, where the spike of a *sal* tree, wrapped by a fold of red cloth rounded off by some white material, stood and the red and white stripes wound to the top, there – shifting her head playfully against an exposed nail – Ruku had heard a song vibrating in the air and sky:

I remember how many days and nights
I was your playmate ...

When Hemant Kumar crooned "*O rock, rock, my heart ...* Ruku had felt her heart palpitate at the soft touch of someone's fingers. Phalgun had been her playmate for so many days and nights! He was so close to her she didn't feel he had a separate identity; she became aware of it only in the evenings when she had to go back to another house. But that house was also nearby. Looking down from her room, Ruku could see pieces of cut-fish, potatoes, and *patol* lying about, clearly visible in the veranda adjoining their kitchen. Only a narrow lane separated the two houses. The house next to hers, in front of the road, belonged to Monimashi. The old one-storey mouldering building behind her was Phalgun's, Phalgun and his mother's. He had no brothers or sisters. "That's why he bullies you like this," Umamashi had told her. Really, the way they had fought – standing in front of the dank lane – when children. Phalgun had pulled her by her hair, got her flat on the ground; Ruku had dug her teeth ferociously into his arms, he had howled and run seeing blood spurt. Umamashi had to pull Phalgun back into the room after giving him two smacks with her *atta*-covered hands. The two had grown up alongside, unified in body and soul. Not quite! Asleep in bed at night, they stuck out their tongues at each other in silent taunt, chuckled in their dreams at something incredibly funny.

Ruku was quiet, timid but sharp in studies, worried sick at the mention of sports. She kept a diary in her school bag all the time. Who could tell she might not feel like penning a poem! Phalgun hated studies, went to school as a habit, egged on by his mother. He didn't care about reading school texts; he got hold of all kinds of story books from the library. He had taken to the violin already when he was in class six. One wondered how a boy like him could stay so quiet when one saw him playing music, sitting by the window all by himself.

But he was an expert when it came to tending the fledglings that dropped out of their nests. He kept a small screwdriver, scissors, nails, candles and glue constantly in his pockets. The little mechanic's pockets were always gummy. Umamashi felt like dying when she had to wash them clean. Phalgun had built a doll's house for Ruku. He was only three years older than her, yet there was such magic in his hands. A shoe-box closed on all sides strung to another shoe-box was a house. Windows and doors were cut out with blades; the two had painted it together and made doll's chairs and sofas by sticking match boxes. Phalgun produced a glass dropper from his own table, pulled off its rubber cap and it became a tube light for the doll's house. Everything was going well ... then a roaring fight broke out betweeen the two about where to sit the dolls and how to dress them up. Ruku plonked the doll's house at the head of the narrow lane, out of temper. It rained heavily on the day of the *Rath:* the doll's house soaked with water turned into a wet rag, Ruku howled. Phalgun stood shamefaced. The two made up amidst torrential evening rain. Ruku ran to his place, unable to stay away, her hands dripping with oil from fried *papads*.

Ruku had come away leaving Phalgun behind. The sadness of parting with Ma, Baba, Umamashi, Mesho, so many other friends is of one kind: a dull pain that wore her down. This was different, like a sharp wedge which made the heart bleed. Will Ruku ever be able to get away from this land of mists and clouds, from its dense coldness, its unexpected rains, its winding roads strewn with pine needles? Will she ever find Phalgun again? And who and what is Phalgun? Is he the boy whose black and white passport photograph lay among the clothes in Ruku's suitcase? Who had held her, enclosed her in so many enchanting ways all this time and wouldn't let her go? He would come to her making outrageous demands; such a lot of trouble when she complied with his requests, such disquiet when she didn't – disappearing at one moment, his wild hair flying all over the place, wearing a yellow panjabi; returning the next, roaring with laughter, getting down from a red double-decker with a fisful of papers in his hands; at times the violin would send out melancholy music from the dark terrace.

As if Phalgun was not a person, an individual human being, but an extended picture; an ensemble of smell, touch, colour, emotion – the entire atmosphere of his town and his neighbourhood. He came alive as a landscape in her mind's eye whenever she thought of him. Different shades of colour, objects, hazy faces of people and so many other things fixed and illumined by sunlight or seen through the filtering radiance of the chinese lantern. A big river or the long stretch of hills, dreamy tableau of times past, the patter of familiar feet keeping time with the assured rhythm of a slow passenger train ... can one person symbolise so many things all at once, mean the moonlight, the sun ... all of them? Ruku hadn't realised that earlier, she thought about it now.

Phalgun was gathering momentum in her thoughts, slowly encompassing an ever-widening realm since she had come away, leaving a part of herself behind. Here she knew no one, the rhythm of her life had undergone a drastic alteration. Here the language, inflexion, the mode of address were all too different. Phalgun loomed large in her consciousness like the star-studded sky and the light that radiates in between dark polarities, filled her up to the brim. There was hurt, like an exposed wound coming into contact with the finger, if she so much as tapped those corners of the mind which were her very own, which she was compelled to leave behind. The boy had accompanied her to the end of the road-away-from home with a smile on his face, had looked so confident and happy when he said "You'll come back here, won't go anywhere." His face floated in the yellow-green of the sky whenever she turned to look at it.

There was a gunshop beneath the entrance to the building, festooned with dirt and cobwebs. Splashes of rain flailed her body. Ruku felt tired standing out of doors. She was wary, her mouth dry; she was tongue – tied and nervous. The results of the Civil Service exams had been declared; inside were names of those who had been selected. A lot of shouting went on around the notice board inside the rickety building. Phalgun had gone in making her wait outside. As soon as he came out, frightened Ruku asked, "What did you see ... have I got ... through?"

"You have sailed through. Now go and see with your own eyes, you cowardly creature!"

Walking home along the rain-washed streets they had noticed tramcars moving as if blindfolded with the word End written on boards stuck to their front. How can the front suggest End? The city lights had come on by then – Calcutta had become a sea of human beings returning home. The trees, wet with rain, looked slick and green. Within herself there was a sense of deep exhaustion, and consonant with it an excitement mingled with sadness. Phalgun had walked by her side without uttering a word. "You won't go anywhere ... you'll come back here." Ruku had been hanging on to those words since the day before.

The library was in the basement, huge, spreading its wings on either side. Emerging from the dining hall one came slowly down the red-carpeted staircase. A carpet covered the wooden stairs; there was the danger of a sprained ankle if one was not careful. The entire front portion of the library was encased in glass. Because of its situation, well below the level of dining hall and lounge, you could look deep into the dense forest of the tableland, colourful pine trees and the faraway mountains.

When the mist rolled down and blotted out the scene, then the glass-encased library appeared like an island or a room of chandeliers and all around it the enchanted sea. "You won't go anywhere. You'll remain mine." Ruku clung to those words with all her emotions.

Entering the library after dinner on her first day at the place, Ruku had felt fear and cold smothering her like fog. "Where have I come?" she had asked herself. "In which world? Where's Ma? Phalgun?" The smell, the clamour, the cry of hawkers of Harish Mukherjee Road seemed to have fled, vanished into thin air and Ruku, alone and abandoned, was a little bird desperately combing the vast expanse of air unable to find the signpost of her destination.

Ruku lifted her head from the pillow at the faint sound. Two drops of dried up tears stained the pillow: traces left behind without her knowledge. Kusum was combing her hair, getting ready to eat. She had possibly taken the casette out of the cassette player; her spirit seemed free of all misgivings. Ruku put on her walking shoes the minute Kusum's red anchal fluttered and disappeared behind the heavy curtains. She was supposed to go and meet Kuldeep's parents. Eight already! Goodness, it had got so late, the two old people must be waiting for her to arrive and not taking their food. Ruku scurried down the stairs and ran towards Gobinda Pant Hostel taking the near-dark, halogen-lit road.

The Block is one of National Academy's oldest. Below, it is a portico bounded by pillars, and to its far end a huge lecture hall. One comes upon a number of guest rooms on the first floor as one goes through the hall. An old steep staircase makes for the student's block on the second floor. Ruku had been compelled to stay a few days at that terrible place, haunted by all kinds of ancient ghosts when she arrived. She heard strange sounds through the night, the *thak thak* noise of wooden stilts pacing the terrace, sounds of shrill whistle piercing in through gaps in shutters. She was already unhappy, having to cope with the hardship of the sudden ascent into higher regions and the bitter cold. Chill descended from the high cracked ceilings. She shivered underneath a single blanket all night. The warmth from the room-heater hardly got as far as her bed. Afterwards room mate Rinchen had quipped. "So many blankets in the cupboard ... why didn't you take some?" By then it was morning, her arms were already slightly warm from the snowy-white gleam of sunlight on the icy peaks.

All the guest rooms had locks hanging on doors. Perhaps no one was in and the guests out for dinner. One door was slighly ajar – sounds of laughter reverberated from within. Kuldeep exclaimed as soon as she peered in, "Look Rukmini is here! Navroj, let her have the chair."

Navroj pushed it towards her and sat on the bed. Two single beds were placed side by side in the room. The old woman who sat on one, her head covered, a shawl over her sweater and who was now making Ruku sit down, smilingly placing her hand on her head, was Kuldeep's mother. His father was seated on the only other chair with arms. He looked passed seventy, had frail hands emaciated with age.

"Ma and Babuji have arrived from Thiog," Kuldeep

anounced.

"Do you know, Ma, I am teaching Ruku Punjabi." He went on, "Come on Ruku, repeat what I taught you the day before yesterday."

"What are you up to Kuldeep? "Ruku knit her brows.

Kuldeep got up and sat behind his mother, resting his thick-bearded chin on her frail shoulders. The stinging smell of liniment hung in the air. His mother smiled. "I hurt my fingers getting into the train ... they are a bit swollen, that's all." Ruku held her hand and gently stroked it. Small and infirm it had had to cope with so many domestic chores. Five sons, countless brothers-in-law, lord knows the amount of wheat she had had to pound for her sister-in-law's family, the many puffy *rotis* she had had to take out from the deep of the oven. But hadn't she too gazed at mist-filled evenings descending upon the mountain range close by when she went to milk the buffaloes? A discoloured nose-ring adorned her nose; her shapeless, ordinary *salwar-kameez* carried a mild smell which sent out intense ripples as the bodies of all mothers do.

"Are you comfortable here ... what about the food?"

Kuldeep answered, rocking his body from side to side, before Ruku could open her mouth. "So uncomfortable, suffers terribly, she wants only rice and fish curry – rice and curry – runs at the sight of *rotis*."

"An absolute lie," Ruku shouted. Actually she felt like fleeing every time she came across South Indian food: *idli*, *rasam*, *sambar* and she had to gulp that hot, sour, salty stuff *ad infinitum* ... The fish brought from Dehradoon was like some fossil. Who knew they weren't *Koyelakanth*, dug out from the deep freeze of Dehradoon mountains, a prehistoric fish? Eating fish with Dehradoon rice Ruku felt homesick for *Hilsa*, or *Khoera*, for red spinach or the poppey-seed paste delicacy. She had a ding-dong battle with Kuldeep when she tried to translate into Hindi the names of those recipes.

Kuldeep's father spoke out in a rather serene voice, "Come over to our place when it gets less cold – around February-March – you'll see so many flowers there. You can eat apples, pears, walnuts to your heart's content. Snows melt and run down the mountain ridges. You'll see the ice-covered peaks in all their glory."

Kuldeep's home was like a farmhouse, built out of bricks with a corrugated metal sheet as roof. Ruku had heard that the route to Thiog gets frozen during winter. Ice drizzles at the beginning of the cold season; the steps disappear under a white blanket. The glass shutters of the yellow house get fogged, become a blur. Close by the Himalayas sparkle in sunshine; sun falls on sharp clefts in the hard ice, reflecting the blue sky in the colour of rusty steel. The pink flowering cherry trees stand against the sky. The air is without any reverberation, so still that one can make out the chirping of each and every bird.

Kuldeep said, "Baba has become so quiet, terribly uncommunicative since my brother's death. He supervises work in the farm, fetches fruit and vegetables to the market by himself, hardly smiles. My elder brother was in the army, Col. Harmeet Singh." Kuldeep's eldest brother was older than him by fifteen years. A splinter from a bullet had got stuck in his spine during a shoot-out in the North Western frontier. He had been paralysed from his chest down. It left him immobile, turned him into a stone at the age of thirty-two. He had lain in bed in the farm and had looked at the sky and the mountain range, while the adolescent Kuldeep and sister, Gurpeet Kaur, read out newspapers to him.

He had stayed alive like this for eight more years, then Death glutted itself on him, taking him by his neck, throat and lips. His wife stopped visiting her family after that. Her father, an old Jat farmer and a childhood friend of Kuldeep's father, still came over to them in his bullock cart to discuss sundry matters. The sister-in-law was terribly fond of Kuldeep. She cried piteously the day he left home to go for his training.

Kuldeep had seen his mother and sister-in-law hanging the washing on the clothes line in the plot of land behind their house, some months before his elder brother died. His sister-in-law was in tears. She looked dejected and mother was telling her in a tranquil voice, "Parminder, steel yourself. A tearful face doesn't become people whose sons go to the front." Kuldeep's gentle mother, such mental strength she had! She had single-handedly looked after father, Kuldeep, her daughter-in-law after his brother had gone. She would say, "Look at me ... I am still upright though I have lost some one tied to my umbilical cord."

Bearer Dhanpati came with a tray of food for Kuldeep's parents. "You two eat ... we are going out for our dinner",

Kuldeep said, coming out of the room taking Rukmini and Navroj along. Seen from the shaded precincts of G. B Pant hall, the zigzaging brilliance of the lights of the lounge can be bewildering. The lounge is so enormous that at first Ruku thought she had come to the bright spectacle of an airport; all the buzz inside its hub didn't penetrate beyond its glass walls. From the entrance she could notice fingers waving, the movement of painted lips, neat, dignified heads sitting comfortably on top of the blazer collars – a mime play seen from a distance. Shoes sink into the wall to wall blue carpet, there is old furtniture made out of mahogany wood, with ornamental glass-topped tables placed in-between. A second glass door opens out to a secluded balcony at the opposite end of the lounge.

There – behind the wrought iron railings – one can see the rolling highlands, the pebbled road meander below rows of pine and deodar trees and wind its way to the villages. Now the hilly pleats are dark.

Murals covering the two walls of the lounge depict the story of India's struggle for independence – from the Mutiny to 'Quit India'. Men fighting enveloped in flames, men raising their fists to the sky holding the flag high, men falling on the ground, men dead. However much the heat in the flaming pictures, it doesn't get to the body; instead the murals fling the feel of cold. Ramlall had made a tiny shop out of the small corner behind the door at the other end. Such a little place, it was amazing how he could store so many long-playing and 45 RPM records there; he also had cigarettes, loose and in packets, matches, chewing gum, peppermints, all kept in glass jars. Ramlall put on your favourite record if you just sent him a chit.

While at dinner, Ruku's heart suddenly quivered and a piece of potato fell into the chicken sauce. Rafi's voice – its ardour and the longing – blasted her senses: *Chowdhibike Chand ho, ya aftab ho, jo bhi ho tum, khuda ki kasam lajawab ho.*" Veils lifted one after another – hair tumbling all over the shoulders, two eyes like monsoon clouds or a cup of wine full to the brim, lips suddenly bright with play – that incomparable beauty whose path the firmament of stars stoop to kiss, the unequelled she for whom music rebounds on the walls and the ceiling and waves over to the balcony – does *lajawab* mean incomparable in Bengali?

"You are beyond compare, matchless – remember that." Was the person who had put down those words in the corner of a letter looking for someone like the object of that heart-rending song? But Ruku has none of her qualities. She is so commonplace, ordinary, like the *dure* sari, or perhaps she has something unusual in her, to discover which she'll have to engage herself in a lifetime's search. When daylight wafting over Banarpuchha and the peaks of Vasudev enters her room Ruku stands in front of the mirror and looks at herself, inspects her eyes, her forehead, her waist-length long black hair and the faint shadow under her lips and thinks, "It's a mystery what Phalgun sees in me ... I will probably never know."

"Hey, you there! Goodness, the Bengali poetess is lost in reverie!" Archana Agarwal broke into peals of laughter standing behind her. Ruku stirred. She felt rather embarassed, the raisins in the milk pudding were leaping to her eyes, she took a bowlful and placed it on her plate. The queue was long. It had turned the corner and got stuck because she hadn't moved. People with plates in their hands, stood fixed, how terrible! Ruku quickly found a table and sat down. Navroj followed suit.

They could see Kuldeep coming from a distance, laughing. He must have made a round of Ramlall's shop, for almost at once Shib Kumar Batalvi's ghazal reached a crescendo, "I am captive to your charms, *mainu tera shabab*." Kuldeep had taken her in hand and explained the particular meaning of the line.

When she had first heard Punjabi spoken, Ruku had thought it sounded like pebbles rattling inside a small tin, especially the talk of her Kalka train companions. Now she had got used to it. Now when Kuldeep and Navroj talk to each other, or when Himmat and Darbar, shouting on top of their voices, join them from the faraway lit up corner of the road, during an evening walk, Ruku thinks she is listening to the waves of the strong united voices of the rural people, who haven't buckled under the situation inspite of the beatings they had had to endure during the Partition. The clatter of their feet mingles with the discordant sounds of tractors on the go.

On other days the lawn is flooded with light. The huge bungalow of the Director is adjacent to the building, the brightness of the portico on the first floor falls on the grass. Sankaran was probably away in Delhi on work. A strange man. At times he joins them at dinner with his wife, eats and talks casually. Then there's whispering and a note of warning: "Diro,

Diro," they refer to all Directors by that dimunitive. But Sankaran is from Kerala and different from all others. Is he a misfit there, in the land of mowed lawns, blue carpets, bone china and immaculate clothes? The boys and girls from St. Stephens and Miranda House shrugged their shoulders when Sankaran simply got rid of the barbaric protocols of formal dinners. Dress codes and table manners were printed and distributed at the commencement of every dinner occasion : instructions about how to make a toast, wishing good health to the chairman or a special guest at the beginning of a dinner. How to stand up without unsettling the tablecloth or upturning a chair – the torture! Ruku found herself facing one of those terrifying evenings when there was a formal dinner to bid goodbye to Director Chopra. She was obliged to escort an appointed guest and sit on the chair alloted in the printed plan exactly a minute and half before dinner. Ruku got into the wrong queue, looked back and perspiring profusely, asked her guest "Could you tell me where chair number three, MB is?" Joint Director Srivastava gave a severe smile and said "Miss Banerjee are you escorting me or me you?"

Ruku found her feet getting continually entangled in her silk saree. Flimsy Murshidabad silk had hardly any distinction. No girl in the place wore such cheap silk – brocade, Mysore silk and Kanchipuram sarees were the rage, especially on nights of formal dinners.

The leaflet of table manners had such 'out of the world' do's and don'ts.

1. One had to get into the chair from the right side to sit,

come out from the left.

2. One must talk only to the person sitting on the left during meals (but if the person to the right talks?)
3. One must not use cutlery meant for roast chicken for eating fish; there's different cutlery for fish.

Jaipur's Kushal Mathur had drawn two cartoons after going through the booklet: a big fat fish with knife in one hand and fork in the other with the heading, "Fish has its own cutlery". Another cartoon showed a giraffe twisting itself to get into the chair from the right side and coming out squeezed thin. Kushal had studied at a moffusil town in Hindi medium. He had then attended the university at Jaipur. He was skilled at drawing cartoons. The Stephanians scrutinized his cartoons solemnly. When Sankaran abolished fish and its accoutrements from dinner then the thought of the future of 'India that is Bharat' sent shock waves in hostel rooms and lounges.

Anurag Srivastava had declared, "Ladies and gentleman, get used to the good life... then only will you know how to remain in comfort in the huts of poor farmers".

But if the first half of the instruction becomes too easy to follow and we forget to learn the other half, we? what then? Ruku thought to herself.

Whose India is it? Sankaran had once asked this very question, pouring tea from the teapot at his own house. The problem seemed both simple and complex. One hundred and twenty five girls and boys were being trained for the huge stretch of this country, for Bihar, Orissa, Betul, Chhindwara, Peryar, Kohima and the Andamans. They were being gradually prepared in a big cauldron of horse-riding, yoga, physical training, lectures, seminars debates, group presentations, film shows, social service and field trips among others and then sent out to villages in a state of dire poverty, or in abysmal darkness, rivers with falling banks and health centres without doors.

Would Mansoor from Lucknow, in the pink of health or Tara of Delhi who gets mad with anxiety if her nail polish doesn't match her salwar, or Priya from Madras who only goes to four star restaurants because she cannot digest coarse rice or unhusked lentils, be able to comprehend the language of the common people?

Actually if one had to come to this ivory tower in the nest of clouds – to the cuckoo land – one had to fulfil so many conditions: be smart in studies, in games and general knowledge. But half the game is lost if one's medium is not English – English so necessary not only for speaking, but to sneeze, to cough, to take an oath. Did Ruku know that? Girls and boys from English medium schools had one foot on the ladder to Heaven already from their childhood. The Rukus of this world played *kit-kit, ekka-dukka* standing far below them. They dreamt of arriving at the ivory tower, crossing the dusty grounds of Jagabandhu Institution or Sabitribala Vidyalay, catching the Dehradoon Express or Kalka Mail from the Howrah Station. How ridiculous can one get!

The girl in the *dure* saree had trudged thus far by virtue of her brilliant results, yet Ashit Kumar, a simple B.A. from Kurukshetra University, who had scouted for coaching institutions and taken tutorials, surpassed Ruku with ready-made answers to questions posed. She was amazed – all this training, laying down a foundation for future activity – wasn't it taking them further away from the people of this big country called India, who they might serve? How could Tara, Ashit or Mansoor come out of their enslavement to health, to smartness, glib talk, and the oblique and indifferent arrogance encouraged by their social situation?

To prefix the word 'idealist' to Sankaran's name is merely to abuse him for defying societal norms. Where's the scope for idealism these days? Sankaran was carrying on a lone battle for all he believed in so that accountability found a place in the system. He was different from others, simple in habit and dress, quiet, yet dogged to the extreme. He had served in Bihar whence political fury hounded him from district to district. He accepted innumerable transfers from one department to another, but didn't give up his resolve. "They know that if compelled, I can return to my village in Kottayam and take to farming", Shankaran had laughed and said while taking a special class with Ruku and her friends. "You can't pressurise people who have nothing to lose".

"Is the new `Diro' a commie?" Atish Jha jumped up, fists clenched at Mansoor's remark. And why not? Atish had a long record of student agitation at JNU, a profile for which he had to approach the Home Ministry to escape harassment during police verification. It was natural that he would fly off the handle at mere mention of the word "commie" His face was red, veins on his forehead about to burst.

Sankaran was away in Delhi. There was no light on the grass from his window. Ruku felt isolated, terribly lonely in the evenings, these days. He lived so high above, in quiet solitude yet he seemed to have touched a chord in her heart, invisibly from a distance. That was unbelivably true. Whose India was it? Ruku walked along the side of the darkened lawn and wondered all by herself. Others walked, in couples or in groups of three, the usual 'after dinner,' leaving behind the post office, crossing the deserted uneven, craggy road, towards the gate flanked by sodium lights on either side, then walked back. Some went off to the corner canteen to eat *gulab jamuns*.

Navroj was standing quietly on the right end of the lawn with his hands in his pockets. Kuldeep had got hold of two or three others. They would walk. Ruku felt sleepy. She would go home, to the Ladies Block, to her own room. The blue letter lay under the circle of dim light of her table lamp. Phalgun was waiting! She felt drawn – She walked fast. She had forgotten that Navroj hadn't spoken all this while. Navroj won't talk till he can arrange all the questions he would ask of her in his mind. He seemed so naturally genial in temperament, but had a tortuous mind, and got easily offended. He would nurse grudges without revealing them to anyone, and then make them known quite unexpectedly through a joke, when the atmosphere was sunny; like the thorn that sticks under the feet when walking over the fallen pine leaves.

Navroj stood with his back against the cold railings as dew settled on the dark valley behind. The windows of the small huts of bearers and porters were shut to ward off the cold.

Above, the lounge, the dining hall and the hostels stood out in the dark like so many radiant islands. The people of those islands don't know what unmitigating darkness is – they will, however, experience it all through their lives.

What could be Navroj's thoughts now? He would be thinking of the mountains covered with a thick sheet of ice, of heat and smoke issuing from the caves of Jwalamukhi Temple, of ice-coated roads, the courtyard, and the chill inside the kitchen, hardships. Baba had become so difficult, wouldn't talk, because his son had gone so far away for his studies. Ma was no longer there, she was no more. Navroj more than any other person knows what her absence means, the loss, the loneliness. No other person ... his aunt, his uncle especially his father. He had so much to tell her, now those words will remain unspoken, forever.

Rukmini was progressing towards her yellow lamp-lit bedroom. The almond-colour eyed Kuldeep was pressing on, laughingly. Navroj's lips were pressed tight; he was on the verge of tears. To him the sky reflected the imaginary features of another face. He knew that no matter how far he travelled, and whatever long distances he covered he would never, ever feel the touch of those soft white hennaed hands – or see a smile that resembled the movements of the pale green waters of the river Beas.

TWO

The road branches off in three different directions as it moves down from the huge concrete arch where the words 'National Academy' are boldly engraved. After a slight drop, the path to the right makes a steep ascent, encircling the hills and going all the way up to the library point. A corresponding one meanders leisurely in the direction of the company gardens; still another fronting it slants downwards, losing its track in the tarred road next to the riding ground. There, below the terraced hills, are shops – a grocery, a laundry and one other selling soaps and cigarettes – doing brisk business. Ramesh's shop styled as canteen, although no noticeboard by that name exists, is actually a one-room affair. But you can get everything there, from toothpaste, squash rackets to *pan parags* and birthday cards. The place is crammed with goods lined up on parade. The light is too dim to make things out immediately – one gets used to that sooner or later.

Those who are exhausted by the din and noise of Calcutta, Bombay and Madras markets become restless with craving when they see the stationery goods on sale in the blurred darkness of the still mountains. The veranda is L shaped with a tin roof resting on wooden posts. There is a canteen there – a table draped in a white tablecloth and a row of chairs. A stove is kept burning in the tiny kitchen at the back. Ramesh's wife fries *parathas*, stuffed with potato, radish or spinach; in *asli* ghee. It was five in the evening: girl and boys, a whole gang of them, were at the table, ordering hot coffee, some of them asking for hot *pakoras*. Boys from Bihar, Punjab, Haryana and Madhaya Pradesh go for *parathas* made out of *desi* ghee; the girls, no matter where they come from, are extremely weight conscious. They only nibble at pieces of *parathas* and refuse to eat.

Sounds of the gentle movements of Ramesh's wife and the swishing noise of her *salwar-kameez* can be heard. Soon a fair hand would hand out plates, one by one, and Ramesh or his servant boy would arrange them on the table. Ramesh gave as much care to this job as he did when he displayed the new list of Penguin books to the girls and boys.

Those bent on slandering him swear Ramesh had arranged

the marriage of his three daughters with would – be administrators by feeding them with *parathas* There was no tangible evidence that this was indeed the case, no one had ever seen his married daughters or his sons-in-law, for that matter, appear at the table.

The evening darkened. A lot of gossiping was going on at the table in one corner of the veranda. Rajinder Singh was saying something, thumping the table. Venkatesh was looking at him with tranquil eyes, taking off his specs. Sunila Oram was sipping coffee, reading a book. All of them made a big fuss and beckoned to Swarup when they saw him come out of the store. Swarup was a late entrant of the Academy, fair and shy; he blushed at the sight of girls. He was late in joining the institution as he had had to leave a previous job. And it had taken him sometime to overcome his inhibitions about socialising. A real bookworm! Must have sat poring over books all this while.

"What will you have, Swarup?" asked Sunila affectionately.

"Nothing – I'm full up", Swarup's typical response.

Sunila gave him a hard look over her specs. Sunila was sheeny black, robust, with hair combed straight back and knotted into a bun at the nape of her neck. A tribal girl from Ranchi who had studied in a missionary school, she did not have any misgivings or embarrassment about her complexion. She laughed all the time, revealing a set of sparkling white teeth, eagerly taking part in sports, drama and debates. Although Swarup was normally in full flight at the sight of girls he was totally subdued when Sunila took him to task.

"No-nonsense, sit, I'm placing the order."

"Who dares to give orders with me here, at this table ... Ei Swarup, sit" – Rajinder pushed him into the chair and went into Harish's kitchen. Rajinder was tall and slim with keen eyes, thick unruly eyebrows and a neat moustache. He had no doubt at all that one day he would become a renowned police officer and stamp on the infamous Chambal valley. Rajinder always spoke out with a great confidence, heckled endlessly, taunted and teased people who disagreed with him, shouted and got violent if his arguments failed. Sunila kept reading her book not wanting to aggravate the situation.

Swarup sat on the edge of the chair (that was his style), and looking at Sunila imploringly, mumbled, "Look Sunila, I am sorry!" "Never mind," Sunila turned the page of her book, appearing serious. By then Swarup was gazing tearfully at her, and his right hand stretched across the table was ready to touch her fingers, given encouragement.

"The boy is crazy, so painfully shy ... Sunila, order something for me, see how my stomach has caved in!" Roaring with laughter and thumping Swarup's back Venkatesh sat humpbacked. The atmosphere turned cheerful again with Sunila's and Swarup's laughter. Rajinder was back having placed his order, with Harish in tow carrying the dishes.

The savoury smell of freshly-fried spinach in *ghee* and shredded ginger made Swarup feel ravenously hungry. While breaking the hot *roti* carefully into crumbs so that his fingers didn't burn Swarup realised that it wasn't just the steam given off by food that made all the objects, save for the plate and the table in front of him, appear blurry. But yes, he was always hungry, so hungry that one could say that food was his sole and primary interest in life.

He felt hungry the moment he was up in the morning; a biscuit with bed tea were all he got before the PT class. Hardly was the class over before he was seized with hunger pains that seemed to suck at his entrails like some blotting paper. His stomach was soothed till twelve noon by a double – egg omlette, four pieces of buttered toast with jam, a glass of milk. Again at one p.m., during the Economics or Constitution class, the image of the basement kitchen, where *rajma* spiced with *ghee* was being cooked in huge pans, would float in his mind's eye. Lunch was served between one thirty p.m. and two; by five in the evening his stomach would sound a note of alarm! What a nuisance! And the boy from Hoshiarpur in Punjab had not yet learnt the use of forks and knives like the regulars of this place.

His father was a forest guard. There were four sisters at home, all of them younger than him. His father had been unable as yet to pay off the loan he had taken to buy him jacket-blazer-tie for joining the Academy. Five hundred rupees out of the nine hundred Swarup scraped together every month went towards the mess expenses, his three daily meals. He spent the rest on stationery, paper, pens and pencils and other items of daily use; he bought and kept a packet of biscuits in his room. He liked to leaf through books and magazines in Harish's shop as he never had the means to buy them. That wasn't much of a problem. He could take as many books as he liked out of the library except for the new titles.

Swarup hardly ever sat at Harish's table. He couldn't afford to eat on his own and was embarassed about eating at other's expenses. He simply couldn't return the invitation. A greater problem was that no one allowed him to pay – stopped him by shouting "No, no." His ears would redden when the boys behaved that way, but he felt different when it came to Sunila. His self-consciousness seemed so unimportant when he was confronted by the unwavering look of her pair of black eyes, so full of affection.

Swarup was eating happily, folding bits of *achar* into the *paratha* even as Rajinder and Venkat sauntered out of the room, taking their tennis rackets along. Now only he and Sunila were left at the table. At the next table, boys and girls came in and out. People crowded into the shop. The night was closing in. A cold wind brushed Sunila's cheeks; it made a rustling sound in the shadowy heights of the tall deodar trees. Sunila slowly walked back to her Block, taking the steep road to her right. Swarup trailed behind. He was staying at Green Valley Block. His room was the last one on top of the building, room number seventy-eighty; a wooden staircase taking several turns ended there. The green-coloured wooden peak of the building stood out from top of his room – one could see it from a distance.

As one looked down from one of its windows, the riding ground appeared elongated, oval shaped – a neat, quiet plateau in the middle of the mountain green; no pine needles lay scattered there. The sun dazzled sky pierced the chinks in the wall of trees on a cloudless day. Above were different layers of mountains; some distinct, others obscure. Swarup could see all this on Sundays when he was alone in his room, and the hostels too – Brahmaputra, Padma, Prayag – way below on the other side. A track threaded its way down to the Teacher's Block and the tennis and badminton courts. Those who couldn't wait to get there took this route. Rajinder stayed at Brahmpatra. He and Venkat often came across Swarup when they went along with the others.

The road lights were ablaze, creating an illusion of so many islands among spots of darkness. The road was lined by trees on one side, and on the other, beyond the iron railings, loomed a naked emptiness. The riding ground lay below. Sunila was walking without a sound. All of a sudden she looked back and said, "Swarup, which group have you put down your name for, for the village visit?"

"I haven't made up my mind ... and you?"

Sunila pondered for a while. "I am longing to go to Madhaya Pradesh ... have you been there?"

"No," he smiled weakly. Swarup hadn't been anywhere save Delhi where he had gone for an interview and to Chandigarh where he had come looking for a job. The craggy mountains of Madhaya Pradesh, its rivers, forests, its green landscape and the cavernous mouth of the ravines – all fell like a heap in the front of his mind's eye. Sarup felt as if a huge moss-covered granite, piercing the wintry sky suffused with mist and fog, had come crashing down on his head. From where he stood, the landscape appeared unreal!

"Ok, I'll go to the office tomorrow and put down both our

names, yours and mine."

Ramsharan Mishra was a kindly gentleman. He would take note if some of the trainees wanted to go to the same place and accordingly prepare the list. He had a head full of white hair, a white moustache and spectacles that looked as if they belonged to the eighteenth century. He enjoyed accompanying groups on treks or on village visits. He was very caring and had a sense of fun. So many came together to form couples in this land of dreams and yet the relentless passage of time had thrown so many apart. The romance between a Kayestha boy and a Christian girl lay shattered in the fierce trade-war waged in the marriage market. The Sikh boy flew to Karachi or Geneva deserting his Tamil lady love. The girl's father, who was sharpening his sword in revenge and vowing to make mince-meat of his would be son-in-law, had to enfold his broken girl in his arms and wipe away her tears.

Those who bid Ramsharan repeated farewells with pale sad faces on the day of their departure from the Academy, and sat separately on the double door bus, he would see again many years later. They with their wives and sweethearts, would return to this same place to give a talk or have a holiday, bringing one or two bright children along. Who knew if they would recall another face belonging to the cloud-laden days of long ago! But no one would forget Ramsharan. They would smile and salute him with folded palms, say "Ram, Ram Misirji, how are you?" Standing in the shadow of the deodar trees with the sun zigzaging across his body, Misirji would reply "Ram, Ram, quite well, by your grace!"

Who knew what brings people together, what makes them grow apart? What makes humans happy? Today life may seem meaningless without someone, yet five years from now on that very person may seem so remote – like a black dot in the horizon. Misirji pondered over such mysteries of life observing the dusky evening descend on the flat land. He buttoned his coat tightly and rubbed his palms together. The sun had withdrawn from the ancient mountain range. One couldn't even hear the sound of leaves falling in the still atmosphere. Taking the beaten track, Misirji walked towards his small cottage.

"I will put down our names tomorrow." Swarup's entire being was flooded with an immense joy at Sunila's resolute anouncement. It also made him cringe in shyness. He blushed. Thank goodness nothing could be seen in the dark. Sunila wanted to be alone with him – she had arranged for them to be together; the very thought instantly overwhelmed him. He didn't know what to think, this Swarup – he went on mumbling thanks to himself in a voice that sounded strange even to his own ears.

The road above the riding ground gradually sloped to the tennis and badminton courts on the right and to the two multi-storied hostel blocs, Samrat Asok and Tilak on the left. A flight of steps led to the time-worn green door of Green Valley. Sunila had to cross many roads, climb up and down, to reach her Ladies' Block. The smell of moss-covered earth, shrubs and wild plants hovered in the condensed darkness of the heights. Sunila seized Swarup's shy hand and pressed it against her cheeks. Her smooth, warm, moist paleolithic lips travelled over his rough cold palms like a dream. One-two-three-four unique minutes passed. Then the girl giggled, ran up the stairs and disappeared into the compact darkness. Swarup remained standing, utterly bewildered. Gradually his feet, waist and chest recovered from numbness. The concrete steps above lit up looking as if it were floating in the sodium light. Speedily mounting the steps, Sunila called out "Bye, Swarup – Good night!" No goodnight emerged from Swarup's lips. He could merely wave his hands; he didn't even feel like waving lest the touch of those precious lips dropped off.

Barely out of bed, Navroj was embroiled in an argument. He was plotting to gulp down the bed tea and run to his physical training class to avoid it. Gaekwad Sir was a stern taskmaster. He would make late comers stand on one side or allow them to do PT and not give them attendance mark. G.B. Pant Hostel's old washerman, Sishram, blocked his way. He always arrived at the crack of dawn. A miserably thin, old man; the few strands of straggly hair on his head lay unsteadily on his shoulders. He smiled revealing a set of toothless gums – it made Navroj's blood boil.

"Have the clothes been washed to your satisfaction, Sahib?" Why did he have to ask such unnecessary questions? He has managed to stain the cream-coloured pyjamas with maroon, the white shirt has got patches of colour from lord knows whose yellow saree! The more Navroj fumed, the more Sishram gave a licquorishly sweet smile and said, "Why blame a poor man. If Sahib buys cheap clothes, won't the colours blotch or run? What can I do about it? I'm only a washerman not a dyer." Either the man was extremely cunning or unbelievably stupid and so stubborn! There was gossip that Sishram had come along with the washing and woken up some one during the wee hours of dawn. That youngster had hollered, "Don't knock at the door." Immediately Sishram had leapt over the window and stood in his room and said, "I didn't come by the door, Sir." Sishram must have been considerably younger then but it would surprise no one if he leapt over the window now. His old bones were still so supple.

Sishram collected money at the end of the month and kept the account in his little notebook. He placed his bundle of washing underneath the bed and began to scribble in his book, in his usual fashion. Bearer Phulchand appeared and calmed Navroj down. "Get going, Sahib, I'll manage the old man." Phulchand came from the Chamba region of Himachal Pradesh; Sishram belonged to Himachal too. Both their homes were in the suburbs of Shimla, like Navroj's. The early morning row was like a village spat: simple and spontaneous. Although Phulchand addressed Navroj as Sahib, he regarded him as a bad-tempered boy from the next village. Navroj ran at top speed and climbed up to the PT ground.

Wearing white pants, a white full-sleeved shirt and a white sleeveless sweater, Gaekwad was calling out numbers – one, two, three, four – while rows of hands opened out (like some bird's wings) and closed with a clap on top of their heads. Numbers rolled. Rows of feet marched quickly, came to a halt at the warning sound, relaxed and became motionless as the word 'rest' was uttered. Gaekwad gestured to Navroj to step aside and went on rolling out numbers. Navroj waited, feeling stupid. The whole group was giving him a side-long glance. Urmilla, Basab, Deshmukh were laughing and making faces at him. He quickly slipped into the last row, avoiding Gaekwad's eye and joined the group for a twenty-minute sweat-out. When the drill gave and the group had scattered and left, Navroj flung himself in front of Gaekwad. "Sir, please give me attendance, I have exercised for twenty minutes."

"Humm", growled Gaekwad, much like a tiger. He put a P against his name, tweaked his ear and strode off.

Rukmini appeared in front of him as Navroj walked away laughing his head off. She was dazzling like some rain-washed plant with her yoga dress on: a sparkling white *salwar-kameez.*

"Why are you laughing all by yourself? Why is the tip of your ear red?" she asked. By then Navroj had got over his morning's irritations, last night's too. He felt like talking to Rukmini but there was no time for that. He had to bathe, eat breakfast and run to class. G. Subramanium's 'management method class' was in the first period. Subramanium was a small man with black hair and grey whiskers. Alert as a rabbit, he had a hang-up about time. One heard him say 'too early for the next class' even if one were to step into the classroom one minute past nine and, not just that, a memo seeking an explanation for the delay would reach their respective lockers before five in the evening. Getting three such memos meant forfeiting a day's leave. Navroj pushed away Subramanium's image from his mind. "Come on Ruku, let's go and eat."

A huge happy-looking omlette, lay like a field of golden wheat, on a white, bone-china plate. One lost the joy of eating bothering with the forks and knives. Navroj wanted to startle everyone by plonking himself on the floor and stuffing in omlettes rolled in hot *rotis*. Would he get thrown out just because he wasn't observing the protocols?

"Why were you so sad yesterday? Why were you standing all by yourself?"

Navroj had had a letter from his Aunt last evening. Although he wasn't keen on talking to Ruku about it, he couldn't help telling her. His aunt didn't know how to write; someone in the village had written her words down: "I'm not the least bit happy, dear, such a big house, a huge farm all so empty ..."

This feeling of emptiness was an old one. She had felt like this when he had left home to take up his studies at Dharamshala; he then came to Chandigarh for his MA. He visited his aunt two or three times a month when he stayed at Dharamshala, but less often after he came to Chandigarh. Then he was at home only on long holidays. Yet his aunt continued to harbour the hope that Navroj would come running to her if she asked him. They were so rigid about time in this far-off place, he couldn't get leave even if he wanted. Besides he had a job now, he wasn't a student any more. The wild horse in him had got reined in. He had to bury himself in everyday routine and turn a blind eye to the world outside. His aunt, however, never asked him to give up the job and return home.

His Aunt had had to put up with so much – had to even to this day – what with his frightfully ill-tempered father, though hardly six months a year at home. Along with uncle, he spent the entire winter till the beginning of spring in the foothills with his flock of sheep. He took it out on his aunt whenever he was angry with Navroj. His younger uncle had died young when Navroj was still a babe. His mother fell ill and his aunt had taken Navroj into her arms and hung on to him, as one grasps the tangled undergrowth when drowning. Baba had thought since his aunt didn't have a soul she wouldn't dare raise her voice against her elder brother-in-law. He screamed at her and threatened to throw her out of the house. He shouted, without addressing her by name, "I'll drive out all enemies within this house, betrayers who have turned against those who have given them shelter!" Sitting in one corner of the room, uncle stared with his huge eyes, while he kept cleaning the barrel of his gun. A fierce determination seemed to spread all over his caved – in cheeks and drooping mouth. He didn't utter a word. Aunt's hold over the family had increased with Navroj's growing up. Father's and uncle's authority had slackened. His father knew that he couldn't turn his aunt out of the house anymore. She had found the ground under her feet. That's why he went at her in other ways, like leaving *rotis* untouched, complaining they weren't baked enough or making fuss about the food not being properly cooked. He would taunt her saying, "We'll see how your magistrate nephew takes care of you ... he'll make a maidservant of you."

His aunt never replied to those words only wiped her sunburnt, fair face with the sleeve of her loose *kameez*, scratched up the few grains of wheat that had got stuck among the crevices of their stone floor.

Mother had become very weak. She was lying in bed in theevening, her blue-veined hands sticking out from under the quilt cover. His aunt was immersed in cooking. Navroj, a little six year-old child, had gone to light the oil lamp which lay on the shelf. There was a tattered book beside it. Navroj used to read it hundreds of times a day since there were no other books or any piece of paper in the house. Something fell out of his inexpert hands. It made a sound and uncle came roaring in and stood in front of him with legs apart. He looked so big, so fierce!

"Are you lighting the lamp? Son of an ass, taking a fancy to reading, the poor rascal!"

Navroj trembled in fear and hid his face in his hands as was his habit. Uncle didn't beat him up, merely sat on his heels and put out the lamp with a puff. It was his father who thrashed him, returning from the potato go-down, not bothering to wash his dusty hands. He smacked him hard after he heard what uncle had to report. He slapped Navroj's naturally pink cheeks which cracked easily during winter. Drops of blood appeared on their tender surface.

Aunt came running and took him away even as his father was throwing tantrums and stamping about his hands and feet. Navroj fell into his mother's lap and cried, "I want to read, Ma, I want to read."

Mother held him to her closely with her frail, pale hands and took him to bed. There were tears in her eyes. Theirs was a family of illiterates in a village where nobody could read or write. This was how Navroj's struggle began. With no resources, he continued to wage a battle against the darkness of ignorance. It was easier to move the mountain.

Ma was not taken to see any big doctor. It was not the done thing to take the *bahu* of the house to a big city on a cattle cart or the bus. The village doctor didn't hold out any hopes. Navroj's father wouldn't spend a penny on his son's education even if he didn't exactly prevent him from going to school. His mother and aunt took out their old sarees, *tiklis*, noserings and anklets, one by one from their wedding chests and sold them to neighbourhood wives and daughters.

The primary and secondary schools in Purangathi were seven miles from his house. The boy walked there and back five hours each day, carrying chalks and stone pebbles in the pockets of the wrinkled shirt underneath his jacket. He dropped pebbles on the way as a great lark, and got through the spring and summer months in this pleasant fashion. His aunt made him a waterproof for the rainy season, sticking together pieces of torn plastic. Mountain rains descended in the region without any warning and Navroj got wet. He sat by the coal fire and dried his hands and feet. Winter was long and bitter; although he had gloves and socks on, his hands and feet chilled to the bone through the torn Kabuli chappals. At times the long road lay frozen and became hard as ice. It was then that Navroj had to negotiate his way back carefully so that he didn't slip and hurt himself. That was his lot: a high school and college in far-flung places.

At college Navroj stayed in the hostel and didn't have to walk that much. By then the youthful Navroj, soaked in rain and burnt by the sun, had grown sturdy and tall like some deodar tree. His skin had taken on the colour of copper, his head was full of curly, coppery gold hair. He had grown taller and stronger than this elders; his father hadn't taken kindly to that. Leisurely pulling at the hookah, making him sit by his side pinching his cheeks and poking at his shoulders, his father had said, laughing, "Beauty's badge indeed! you are like a sour apple ... a farmer's son, you should be minding flocks of sheep in distant territories, mounting your shoulder guns, taking your hunter dogs along instead of whiling away your youth sitting at home, buried in books."

Actually, Navroj had wandered away from home when he could barely walk; he had held a rifle in his unsteady hands, though in play, and had commanded the dogs from his father's lap. His father couldn't understand how that same boy had grown so indifferent to the pleasures of nature, and didn't get drawn by the faint, burnt smell the earth gave out. And because he couldn't, he cursed and scolded himself, and wondered who would carry on the family tradition – look after the house and farm when he was gone. He lost sleep over it. And yet Navroj's aunt never asked him to go back. Perhaps she feared he would actually come home if she wanted him to. What would have happened then? His aunt didn't know how to read the dates or days. She had a vague idea of the month and guessed the phase of the moon by looking up at the stars. She thought about all kinds of things in a confused state and wrote, "I think of your mother a lot. She would have been so happy if she were alive!"

The dining hall was empty. Girls and boys were hurriedly leaving the place after breakfast. They would either go for their baths or rush to the next class. A piece of toast lay abandoned on a plate, half a helping of cornflakes was left submerged in another bowl. There was a look of wonder and silent melancholy in Ruku's large, black eyes. Yesterday had been Navroj's birthday. They hadn't done much – she had given him a hand painted card, Kuldeep had put on his Bhangra dance act in the lounge. They had brought over some *rasgullahs*, hard as rock, sweet as poison, from Dehradoon. But the seven or eight of them had gone at each other for a piece. Why was Navroj so quiet since the evening? Did the presence of Kuldeep's parents make him feel home sick?

In fact Navroj had been thinking about a morning seventeen years ago. The image of that morning had revolved continuously in his mind and remained bright and shiny to this very day.

He was nudging his mother to wake up as he was about to leave for school. He was baffled to find she was not up as yet. He tried to force her eyes open, "Get up, get up, isn't today my birthday? I want a pudding today, a real rice pudding." His aunt came and intervened, "Leave your mother alone, dear boy, I'll prepare it for you." Ma had a faint smile on her face but she didn't get up. Baba and uncle were away in the foothills. There was no one at home. The boy hadn't realised that his mother was in the grip of death; her feet were already icy cold, the palm of her hands had become frozen. He had walked back from school dreaming about a bowl of rice pudding especially made with nuts and raisins. The sky was bright blue, the trees looked as if they were painted on a silk-screen. He heard the sudden twittering of yellow birds in grass and bushes. He ran into the house and turned into stone. His mother lay covered with a red shawl from head to toe; tears were streaming down his aunt's sunken cheeks. She looked up with a start. There was fear in her eyes. The stream of life that Navroj had known had turned into an icy pool.

"Do you know, Ruku, how much I have thought about it? It was my bad luck ... I am forever unfortunate. Other people can celebrate their birthdays, make themselves merry, give thanks to the Lord for being born. And my Ma, she left me on my birthday. The black thread of sworrow runs through my life. I have never been able to come to terms with it ... I suffer ..."

A piece of folded paper bounced along desk to desk, from the last row to the first, in the unpunctured silence of Subramanium's time-management class. It travelled, hand to hand, from Vinod Kaul to Satyabhama, from Satyabhama to Lakshmi, then to Dilip and finally reached Navroj. It was a poem in Hindi script, in Ruku's hand. The poem spoke of the soul of the universe pulsating in the poet's blood and of the experience of the self merging into the Infinite.

Screwing his face up, Vinod asked, "Is it a poem by you?" A voice less than a whisper, so that G.S. couldn't hear, said, "It's from *Mukti*, a poem in Tagore's *Purobi.*" She wrote the name

RabindraNath in her notebook and silently held it up to his eyes.

An invisible man was walking down the passage in the middle of the classroom towards Navroj. Soon he would place his hands on his head, stroke his back with his gentle fingers. Ruku had seen him many times – so many nights in the pale moonlight – when the deodar trees and mountains cloaked in shadows blended into the radiance of the full moon. A pair of those serene, compassionate eyes would look down at her – and that forehead! All got engraved in her mind as she repeatedly gazed at the black and white or sepia-coloured photograph. What a lot of pain and suffering, he had taken on himself – how this fragile world, riven with conflict and falling apart had given him a place! Navroj must find solace in that. Ruku's little fist had sought refuge in RabindraNath's grasp when she was a child. *"Rock, rock my heart, let its rhythm mingle with the swaying of your hands."* Phalgun was not around – he would have understood had he been. Ruku couldn't decide how to give comfort or make an unfamiliar person in an alien land forget his sworrows. It would have been good if Phalgun were here. She, herself, had been capable of little besides study since she was a child. She had watched sports from a distance, fearing all the time that her glasses would break. Her specs had indeed broken after a fall during the spoon race. She had returned home with cuts and bruised knees. And that put an end to sports. Writing poems – lying on her stomach in bed in the long afternoons during holidays, in the evenings when school was on – was all that remained. It was Phalgun who had introduced her to the world of poetry.

A fourteen-years-old lad, Phalgun was making a straight bid for the world he really belonged to. Disengaging himself from the trivial preoccupations that take over life, brushing aside all that was irrelevant, Phalgun was absorbed listening to classical music. The B channel of Calcutta radio relayed western classical music every night at ten. That music couldn't be heard in the Calcutta streets; there were no cassette recorders in people's homes. Phalgun had already joined the Calcutta School of Music. His inordinate desire to listen to that music could only be gratified by switching the radio on, sitting alone in the dark room with a dim light overhead. When he was small, his father made him lie on his back, and urged him to listen to music on the radio. Faded memories! but they lay suspended in his blood. Those favourite tunes! He wanted to hear them, over and over again. Since an individual request didn't work, Phalgun made Ruku, Mashima and friends ask for them to be played again.

Ruku rarely got the chance to listen to Orchestral music involving piano, violin, cello and flute. Lights went off early in her house. She had to go to bed by nine as a rule or she couldn't get up early. She heard Phalgun at his violin during the wee hours of dawn – a mingling of notes learnt and those freshly composed – elemental like a picture drawn by a boy about to step into his adolescence, or the cry of a drenched blackbird piercing the clouds on a wet afternoon. Ruku's world was built up, little by little, by such sounds and resonances; these tenderly covered her being as if with a fine down.

Who but Ruku knew that the thin, unruly haired boy, Chittotosh-babu often threw out of class because he couldn't draw a map, was the same who walked to school humming the tune of Beethoven's No 1 symphony? The road to school was shaded with ancient trees as it skirted the railings of a nearby park. Phalgun walked alone, bag strapped to his back, his thoughts greatly lulled by Beethoven's music. The third movement of Beethoven's fifth symphony, that expressed the joy of people undaunted by defeat swelled in his heart while he trudged back from the football ground, after a game in mud and water. Yet it had taken Ruku a long while to understand the process by which Phalgun had absorbed into himself all that music. Songs are based on lyrics which speak of human desire, happiness and sorrow: they easily touch the heart's core. But music composed two hundred and fifty years ago, a creation of distant Europe – how could it overwhelm the next-door adolescent boy she had known all her life? Ruku's astonishment never ceased.

The songs of Atulprasad, of Nazrul Islam and above all RabindraNath were heard all the time, everywhere, at home or down the narrow lane. The locality resounded till late into the night with the evening songs of RabindraNath. Strains of *"Stand before my eyes"* poured in through window shutters as the lamps were lit and the conch shell blown. Phalgun could stand in the balcony of a totally Bengali neighbourhood and easily lose himself in the melody of Bach's *Sleepers Wake*. Only Ruku and Umamashi knew that.

The music of *Sleepers Wake* rings with the feeling of warmth and trust among human beings. From Phalgun's deserted terrace one could see the city come alive with freshly-washed pavements, the street roused to sudden activity. The young boy knew the image in his dreams would soon materialize by the window, wearing a knee-length flowery dress carrying a book in hand. It must ... of that he was certain. She – her eyes full of sleep, tangled, uncombed hair falling all over her shoulders – and him. The two would smile at each other spontaneously and without reason.

The melodies of the *Sleepers Wake* would build an invisible bridge between the two windows, forge a bond that rested on the belief that there were many ecstatic moments in store for them in life – a discovery they made on their own; no other person was privy to it.

Phalgun was unexpectedly surprised one afternoon as he leaned forward to have a look at the long-lined exercise book. He had a temperature and hadn't gone to school. Ruku's mauve-coloured dress was fluttering innocently next to Chitramashi's yellow saree on the first floor of their house. The girl was at school. She was in the eighth class; the annual exams were ahead of her. Phalgun had entered college, over and done with school. A new entrant, he hadn't formed a strong attachment to the institution. And he knew, only too well, that he would never, ever have an attachment to any thing other than the house next door and Ruku. The symphony created by Ruku's face and her words had forever drawn a screen of golden sunlight over the rain-laden clouds. Ruku had written a poem in the afternoon. Actually she had started composing it in the afternoon finishing it round midnight. She had got up at four in the morning to pen the last line, such was her poetic compulsion.

A feeling of melancholy had weighed heavily on Ruku for some days past when all of a sudden she felt a gush of happiness that prized open her locked-up emotions. She wanted to tell Phalgun everything – just about everything. Yet she felt so terribly embarassed about her poems. She could only stride into his room , thrust the exercise book into his hands and leave for school. She had felt his forehead with her soft fingers, making the excuse she was taking note of his temperature.

"Hope my fever doesn't shoot up!" Phalgun had exclaimed jocularly. "What rot ... then don't bother to read it," and she had run and disappeared beyond the narrow lane. Bending over the poems Phalgun imagined the red and black checked bedcover sway all over and around the words. Why – it was similar to the melody he had internalised, its beat, its movement was the same as the famous *'Eine Kleine Nachtmusick'* of Mozart. Where did Ruku come across the rhythm? She had never heard this Mozart. She would have told Phalgun if she had. A little girl wants to turn herself into a wild deer as she is angry with her mother. She crosses the mountains, and breathes in the air from the verdant woods under the saffron-tinted sunlight as she watches the day breaking, sitting by the waterfall in the dark.

In the meantime no one knew where the girl had disappeared to. Her friends kept looking for her in the playground. How could they know that their friend had discovered that life itself was a piece of fun? Actually the girl hadn't forgotten her friends, she hadn't after all turned into a wild deer! But she had reached the moment when to her everyday appeared like a Sunday. Holidays were forever! The road to return to her former state was absolutely closed (for the little child). But can the mother forget the child simply because she has left home, or help shedding a couple of tears on her behalf?

Poetry had crossed into the domain of love. It had left by stages the woody lane glowing under the crimson coloured clouds and entered the horizontal land traversing the valley. The rhythm of that movement didn't belong to the realm of poetry but classical music. Phalgun's temperature had come down some time ago; perspiration made his brows damp. He looked up at the clock. It was half past two, not exactly, two twenty to be correct. The street outside was quiet as if it had fallen asleep. There were no cries of hawkers or noise of grinders of stone mortars. The autumn afternoon seemed suspended, holding back its breath; only a bird trilled a message to the distant skies. It was precisely at this moment that overcoming all contrary pulls, Ruku's verses branching off from their roots entered the innermost sanctuary of Phalgun's being. And within an instant Phalgun discovered Ruku installed in his 'deep heart's core'!

To a seventeen year old lad this discovery could not have been intelligible enough for a clear articulation. The image of love came to him finally through protracted musings during the many long afternoons. When it did he felt suddenly awkward, extremely self-conscious, while a wild joy pierced his heart and love enveloped him like mist.

In the terrace that evening Phalgun told Ruku "What kind of a thing you've gone and done!"

"What have I done?"

"You've driven me to distraction. How did you get familiar with the music of *Eine Kleine Nachtmusick*?"

"I've never heard it, believe me."

"But I have never come across such similarity ... had no idea that verses could match melodies!"

Phalgun stopped. He hadn't uttered a fraction of the words that hovered on the tip of his tongue. The starry sky darkened over both their heads, the intense blue amidst gaps in the stars seemed to regard them both. Phalgun hadn't given Ruku the chance to make a fair copy of her poems. He had run to the bureau of *Sandesh* and had handed them in without telling her anything. Ruku too had forgotten everything about it. The annual exams were on top of her; when they were over and the results out, the quiet week that followed seemed interminably long and pointed in the direction of school. It was holiday time – time to hunt for books to buy, look for brown paper wrappings, go after Ma for a new school bag – time for such things. Winter would come knocking at the door in the evenings and then it would be nice to lie in bed, covered from waist to toe in an old soft shawl and read. The smoke from the burning incense wafted out of the corner of the room, making a somersault and resting underneath the table.

On an evening such as this, Ruku heard a knock at the door and Phalgun appeared like a comet with, magazine folded in his fist. "Get up, get up quick, Ruku see! Call Mashi!" He made such a brouhaha! Baba had not come home. Phalgun spread the musical notation of Mozart's symphony across the bedspread.

If I become a curly-horned wild deer then
I can bound over the sleepy mountains under
the saffron-tinted sky at one go
With a fistful of verdant air ...

Phalgun was reading out the lyric for Ruku and her mother's benefit. He did what he had never before done – hummed the melody.

"Do you know, Ruku, the music comes through a play of words and images?" Ruku fell on her poems. Her poems had got printed earlier, but she had never been so excited. Her young mind told her that their worlds, hers and Phalgun's, had now got linked by a rainbow bridge. It hadn't appeared so transparent to her earlier. It seemed as if she was noticing the clouds brighten up after a spell of rain.

Ruku had observed Phalgun from afar, by the window, resting the violin on his shoulder, the bow in his right hand, his silhouette stark against the backdrop of a serene, silent sky. There were no activities about the place save the flitting movement of Phalgun's hands and fingers. How many times had she sat by him and heard him play! She had been happy, her heart overflowing with music, yet there remained a gap in their perfect accord. Ruku was hesitant about closing that gap. How could she venture into the vast complex world of western classical music? It seemed impregnable as a fortress to her. Where lay the port of entry, how could she cross the several dark, dust laden arches to reach there she thought. The gap had finally closed, rendering their worlds a perfect synchrony. Now the lane separating the two houses had vanished, and all the various shapes, the terrace, the geometry of the place had dissolved into a kind of oneness.

Long ago when the two played with kitchen toys, a ten year old Phalgun had made such a fuss, "Ruku, give me something to eat, I'm hungry." She had become serious, noticing the marks on his fingers while she placed make-believe rice, bits of *Madhabilata* and skin of young plantain fruit (standing for fish) into his hands. "Stay, I'll put on some ointment," she had said. Ointment? Nothing but flower-soaked water!

Phalgun had drawn his hands away, "Don't bother. It's an old wound. It's already healed." The little boy's fingers bore black scars left over from skin gashes. Blood had oozed when he slid his fingers down the string to produce a melody. He was so indifferent to pain in his joy at being able to play. He became conscious when the fingers felt sticky with blood. His clothes were soiled out of carelessness; Umamashi shivered in fear. "You can't play any more ... you're really the limit, driving me to my wit's end." But smiling sweetly, the little rascal had secretely picked up the instrument as soon as his mother disappeared into the kitchen. There was no blood now, only the scars. Phalgun sat on, contemplating Ruku with steady eyes. In his imagination he saw her raise his hurt fingers to her lips. Fingers bloodied from sliding the violin strings.

Three

Houses peeped through gaps among trees as well as a boundary wall streaked with green and mud huts with roofs of timeworn tiles. There was a courtyard where a doddery old person lay on a string cot. It was morning yet nothing stirred. A yellow-black butterfly flitted to and from below the *sajne* tree, winging towards the *neem* and *babla* wood. It was the end of the month of *Chaitra.* The atmosphere had not turned humid and there was still a refreshing breeze that blew in from the forest after midnight.

Further away, the unsown fields lay limp, patiently waiting

for the monsoonish month of *Ashar.* A few goats roaming under the shade of a big tamarind tree, in the middle of the grassland, dreamily came to a stop. Such a bright and sunny morning; it was impossible to feel anxious or apprehensive about anything. Akhlu Singh, a wealthy farmer and member of the village panchayat was swaggering with pride and happiness. Would Akhlu Singh have put a shirt on otherwise, so early in the morning? Not a shirt that belonged to him but his son Dinesh! This would have driven him mad if it had been any other day but this one.

Five or six sahibs, magistrates had come to his place. They had travelled from the district town to the Block and had arrived at Pathargara by government jeep. The BDO had escorted them and left them under Akhlu's protection. Akhlu had to see that they were comfortable in every way; he had to supervise their stay, their work and their visits to the village – everything. But Akhlu didn't have to see to all that alone: the panchayat staff were ready and waiting to do whatever necessary; even the police, the chowkidars, forest guards, *sarpanchs* as well as the old MLAs had been well-drilled and let loose. Among the sahibs were two memsahibs. Who knows what they were like!

The kind of things Akhlu had to experience in the course of his long life! A female magistrate? What a joke! ("How can I tell how they are feeling ?" he wondered.) Wife Sita, old before her time, with a face which had multitude of lines and huge earholes (due to the constant pull of heavy earings), couldn't rest all night out of anxiety. "Hai Ram, hai Ram," she breathed out in sleep, as if two time bombs, ready to explode, had been placed on her head. Lachhmi, Dinesh's wife, on the contrary was over the moon about it and puffed up with pride like a peacock. Getting up early that very morning, she was walking past the cowshed, giggling and lifting her veil to take a look at the memsahibs, when the sound of Akhlu clearing his throat sent her scuttling back to her room.

Akhlu's servant-cum-day labourer, Duni came and put a brass pail on the platform. He carried a few heavy bell metal glasses in his other hand. The milk in the pail was bubbling with froth. Sitting on two ancient armchairs, Mansoor and Rohit Kumar were talking quietly among themselves. Rohit belonged to the Balia district of Uttar Pradesh. He owned a flourishing farm, cows and buffaloes, employed day labourers and farmhands. He had come across many old fuddy-duddies like Akhlu. Now, of course, he was well turned out and a highly educated urban gentleman. He enjoyed talking to the old man.

Mansoor's splendid pair of eyebrows met in a frown. Must he spend ten more days in this god-forsaken place – going to the toilet along the boundary wall or on the banks of the canal and ... no morning papers? Impossible! Mansoor was fair-complexioned with fine golden-coloured hair and keen green eyes. He was well-built and tall. Rohit was short and sloppy with a pimply face, puffy cheeks and hair shiny with oil; he laughed all the time. Mansoor was born and educated in Delhi; he went to a public school and then to St. Stephens. He had been getting ready to enter the foreign service when his father had a stroke, compelling him to join the police instead of the adminstrative service. But people didn't know Mansoor had, previously, failed twice to get coveted posts because he had fallen short by six and ten marks respectively and had had to accept a career in police, like a cornered and disgruntled tiger. Mansoor had no doubt at all that in looks and in talent he was the best among all of them and that fate had robbed him of what he deserved. Galloping on a horse without stirrups or standing in the shooting range and chewing grass his green eyes would gaze steadily at his one goal in life, that is, success!

Mansoor was determined to whip up the country's lazy louts, the karma devotees all around him and build up his own image by crushing the criminals. How could the adminstrators in the civil service – who were fat and ugly, had no table manners and stammered nervously when they spoke English – boss over him all his life. To hell with this! Mansoor sprang up gesticulating, "Oh, no, I can't take this!" Rohit was smiling, holding a glass of foamy milk in his hands. Akhlu took the glass away, feeling nervous. He looked up at Mansoor. "The milk is fresh, Sir, real stuff, straight from the farm cow. The cow was milked this morning. How can you keep up your strength and catch robbers if your don't drink milk?"

Dinesh called out in a trembling voice from inside the room, "Babuji!" That shut Akhlu up. Dinesh picked up the pail and hurried to the other side of the quarters where Ruku and her companions were staying. Dinesh had already come to know how bad-tempered and finicky the sahib called Mansoor was. He had a bad time the night before because he had placed Sahib's shiny VIP suitcase upside down. Then a hole was discovered in the mosquito net; it was quarter to eleven at night. Dinesh had to leave his string cot and face a hollering, striped pyjama-clad Sahib. Lachhmi opened her sewing-kit and brought out a needle and red thread. Dinesh sewed up the hole, making long stiches with trembling hands. Had any male member in the generations of his family ever held a needle? But what else could he do? He would have been ostracized by the whole community if he had sent Lachhmi to do the job. Sahib was such a bad-tempered person, it was better to hold his tongue.

Dinesh went to the back of the building and found Rukmini sitting on the balcony swinging her legs. She hadn't combed her hair and had wrapped herself in a yellow *dure* saree. She had her spectacles on and was holding a pencil and an exercise book in her hands. Rukmini was smiling, gazing at the hazy green in the distance; she smiled some more when she saw Dinesh holding the pail of milk and a glass. "Alright, alright, I'll drink a little of your boiled milk, just half a glass ... but only after a while."

Dinesh was pleased about this amicable arrangement.

Rukmini called out to Mohini without turning her head. "Would you like some milk?"

A half-curtain hung on the door. Inside the room were two cots, one for herself, the other for Mohini.

Mohini was from Orissa but she had grown up in Calcutta and was now engaged to Sudev Kapur; there was much speculation in the main campus at Mussoorie about when they would marry. Sudev, Rohit and Mansoor were staying in a largish room. Ruku's room opened out on to an open courtyard.

The kitchen came after it, then a cow shed and a little patch of kitchen garden. The boys' room stood right at the other end. Perhaps by now Sudev unable to bear the pain of separation from his lady love had crossed into their room, without so much as brushing his teeth! Ruku had got up blushing with embarassment and had come away holding on to her exercise book when he appeared on the scene.

She dared not push the curtain aside or peer in. Who knew what she might see! Dinesh too picked up the pail and went towards his own room, scratching his head and feeling rather stupid.

"What are you talking about? Milk? Are you crazy, baby?" Mohini's sweet drowsy voice was followed by a peal of laughter from Sudev. "Ei, Ruku," Mohini called out again, "Can you ask your milkman for a packet of Wills for me? Please."

Ruku opened her exercise book and drew quickly. In front of her lay a blur of trees and foliage, a creeper winding its way to the kitchen roof and the distant acacia trees. All kinds of configurations, straight and curved lines, tracery, took shape as she drew. "I can't, I'm sorry."

The girl Mohini smoked like a chimney; she was almost a chain smoker. What a commotion she had created in the train journey the night before last! She had been writhing with an acute stomach ache looking as if she were a slaughtered animal when she got up to splash some water on her face. Ruku was afraid that she would fall on her face when she suddenly moaned, "Light me a cigarette, please! I'm not feeling well." Ruku had been sitting on the berth alongside. Seeing her sweaty face contract in pain she had fumbled and taken out a cigarette from Mohini's handbag but couldn't light it. Mohini laughed through the twinges of pain and said, "What a silly girl! How can you light a cigarette without putting it in your mouth?" Ruku had managed to light the cigarette finally after pushing it into Mohini' mouth with trembling hands.

It was difficult for Mohini to smoke in front of people in the backward village of Pathargara. She had been warned by the Academy several times not to behave in any way that might make people panic or feel uncomfortable. Cigarettes too were scarce. Sudev hadn't picked up the habit of smoking although Mansoor smoked. Mohini's stock of cigarettes lasted while they were in the district headquarters. She then borrowed cigarettes from Mansoor or tried to get some for herself making him an excuse. Last night Mansoor had clearly told her she couldn't raid his stock any more. "I won't get any for you either ... why smoke if you can't do it openly?"

Sudev felt Mansoor was jealous. Mohini, after all, was extremely pretty. She had large dreamy eyes, a straight nose and a knee-length long plaited hair Why should Mansoor, like an innocent lamb, bring her cigarettes when she flirted with Sudev in front of him, smiling and swinging like some Swarnalata?

"Not to worry ... I'm here, I'll sort something out." Sudev gently let go of Mohini's hand and went out of the room.

Today was the day for their field trip. They would be hitting the road, visiting the houses of small and big farmers, the landless labourers, the adivasis, village mechanics, and the workers of small factories – one by one – taking their exercise books and questionnaire forms along. They would be sitting with them and getting to know them; they would be filling up the forms with their replies. The five of them had to complete two hundred and fifty of these forms with the necessary information about a single village. The group leader would prepare his report extracting essential features of the two hundred and fifty families' life-experience. The report would be analysed in thorough detail when they got back to the district headquarters and comments would be made on the substance of twenty five such group reports. Therefore, six days of field work lay ahead of them.

Mohini had spread her light coloured gold-bordered cotton saree on the bed and a matching nailpolish next to it. She always suffered from nightmares about not being able to match nail polish with the clothes she would wear and worried that if they didn't match someone would notice and think she had no colour sense. An array of different coloured nail polishes were lined up on top of her saree.

The kind of problems people had! Ruku was amused ... it was time for her to have a bath. Two pails of water from the well were kept in a small space enclosed by a half-boundary wall. That was their bath house! She hurriedly gathered up her clothes and soap. Above – the open sky shone brightly, the distant woods and the little houses had become visible. A raven was perched on the branch of a *neem* tree. Yellow and green leaves were floating in the bucket of water. Ruku felt slightly embarassed about taking off her clothes; she was so used to a proper bathroom with a roof overhead.

No, there was no one about – except for the jet-black raven. It seemed as if it was craning its neck and looking at her. It peered at her once with its right eye, then with its left, saw the thin chain glistening round her bare neck and her thick shoulder-length hair hanging loose. As it flapped its wings and glided up into the sky, Ruku's image now appeared blurred to its eyes, dazzled by the brilliant sunlight and melted into the morning glare.

Ruku went back to her room drying her wet hair; she had wrapped the saree somehow around herself. Lachhmi had left her breakfast ready on a stool: a plate of hot *rotis*, a bowl of vegetables, a little bit of *achar* on the side and that horrible glassfull of hot milk. Apparently Dinesh hadn't forgotten! Mohini's food was lying on a chair, covered. There were no tables in the house. Mohini looked grumpy and upset. Her *kurta pyjama* lay on the bed. The saree and the nailpolish were nowhere to be seen ... put back into the suitcase, perhaps. Lachhmi appeared a bit crushed. Her face and eyes brightened up when she saw Ruku.

The girl had arrived at the crack of dawn, even before the birds stirred, and had knocked at their door. Ruku had got up quickly but Mohini, who had been chatting to Sudev late into the night, was still sleeping sweetly. Ruku went out of the room taking Lachhmi along with her, seeing that although Mohini had started off asking for cigarettes gently politely enough, she had gradually got crosser and crosser. Walking by the side of unsown paddy fields they came across a delightful little stream.

Mohini's not getting hold of cigarettes made their situation rather complicated. The day had already advanced, all the people were up and about. Could Mohini take to the fields now? The village maidens and wives had to wait till dusk to venture out to the river banks. "These clowns. They have arranged for everything ... couldn't they have built a toilet?" Mohini asked irritated.

"Ahh! Mohini stop, will you! "Ruku was frowning. Thank goodness, Lachhmi didn't understand a word of English. Puckering her brows Mohini asked whether Sudev had brought cigarettes for her. "He said he would ... what's happened to that?" As if it was Ruku's job to find an answer! Suddenly Lachhmi's face lightened up; she had caught on. She came quickly and placed the four packets of cigarettes, she had been carrying tied to her waist cloth, on the bed.

"Bravo! what a courageous girl!" Mohini laughed away like an actress for a few seconds. "But Dinesh is a fool to have given them to her instead of Sudev.

It's not Dinesh but you who are stupid, Ruku thought to herself. She had been extremely impressed by Dinesh's powers of observation.

"The sun is already hot, get ready quickly or else you won't find a single person at home." Ruku spoke out loudly. Work for six days running – the village had been divided into three segments by an appropriate guess. The five of them would form two groups and prepare questions and answers and write the report. A visiting faculty from Mussoorie would join them for three days to supervise their work.

"What are you up to? Get ready!" Ruku took Mohini's papers out of the bag and placed them on the cot.

But Mohini showed no signs of getting up, She yawned and stretched and throwing her arms about said in a deep voice, "I have changed my group ... you'll go with Mansoor. Sudev and I will form a group."

"But you haven't said anything to me about that! No need to see if I agree, eh?"

Ruku turned around. Mohini and Sudev in one group meant, like now, Mohini would remain in bed till nine – whiling away time smoking – while Sudev Kapur, like a good soul would carry her load and do double the work. As for going about with Mansoor ... that would be another kind of torment! The wily, ambitious Mansoor was always seething in anger; like a snake covering itself with its own venom. To Ruku he was like some scorched summer sand bank; she feared the soles of her feet would get scalded if she stepped onto it.

"Ruku dear, please be reasonable. You know that Sudev and I want to be by ourselves – stay together. Won't you make this little sacrifice for us?"

"Of course I will ..." Ruku slung the bag on her shoulders and left the room without glancing back.

A huge commotion was taking place outside.

Akhlu Singh's house was big and extended. A raised cemented platform ran its full length in front of it. One could say that there were two platforms instead of one as a heavily carved wooden door stood in its middle, through which one crossed into the courtyard. There were four consecutive rooms adjacent to the courtyard which formed the interior of the house. The kitchen, the cowshed and an unusual little room made out of mud came next – that was Ruku and Mohini's room. In spite of its close proximity the men's room was not attached to theirs. The BDO had, apparently, given much thought and scrutinised the house's weaknesses and strengths before he decided to take it. His next job was to make Akhlu agree wholeheartedly to the idea of putting them up.

Today a large group of distinguished people had gathered on the platform outside the house. A thick brew of *elaichi* tea was being prepared exclusively from milk, a fistful of tea leaves and a sprinkling of cardamum seeds. Anurag Srivastav, the faculty member, had arrived to supervise their work. Mansoor, Rohit and Sudev sat innocent-faced, pen and paper in hand. Swapping of stories, *addas* continued. The officer in charge of the police post had also come along, leading to much speculation and gossip in the village. Anurag Srivastava was amusingly relating a few choice incidents from his training period to Akhlu. He resorted to English words often and Akhlu mistakenly laughed at all the wrong places. Srivastava jumped up excitedly seeing Ruku appear. "Ready already? Excellent! Where's Mohini?" Sudev sprang up, and was about to rush to Mohini, learning she was still in bed, when Sriastava gestured at him not to go. One had to be circumspect about what one can or cannot do when in a village.

Some days after Anurag Srivastava had to leave for another district town and for another village. He had to be on his rounds continuously for fifteen days and then send his report to the National Academy. Like Mansoor, he too had felt like a trapped mouse. In that place. No tea in bone china cups in the mornings, no corn flakes! He could get chicken soup at the district headquarter only if he ordered in advance. He had frequently rung home, especially when he felt very despondent. His wife and children shuddered at his plight, and gave him umpteen advice:

"Don't eat food off the streets, be sure to drink boiled water ... take care papa, take care." What a relief it would be when field duty came to an end, he had thought to himself.

One evening, an exhausted Ruku sat on the crumpled bedsheet and started sorting the completed forms. She had rushed about the entire afternoon till one p.m. and had just got back. The food offered to her in various places was not always something she could digest; at times she found it too hot. No Calcutta person's stomach was fit to absorb all that *atta*, *arhardal* and *bhindi*. Akhlu's wife, her head constantly covered, never ceased to invite her to taste one or other such delicacies. She heard the tinkling of Lachhmi's glass bangles, the sound of her movements outside. Ruku had always sat for her meals last in the row, facing the kitchen, where from, time to time she had caught the gleam of a smile in Lachhmi's face. She felt so tender-hearted about everyone; she couldn't get up leaving her plate of food uneaten in a mess. Mansoor and Mohini were capable of that. Those who were experts in table manners at the Academy didn't feel the need to extend normal courtesy to the farmers when they visited their homes. A small nap after an afternoon meal was what Ruku had been used to, but even that was not her fate in this place. Sukdev could be found courting Mohini either sitting on her bed or lying half-reclined. She had to stay outside with a book. It suited Mohini, no doubt. She was never called in. By four in the afternoon Ruku was again out of doors.

Mansoor was most unwilling, made all kinds of excuses for not going out. Ruku found it extremely irritating to go on urging him. At the most, he kept standing sullenly next to the boundary wall of a person's house and remained mum. It was fortunate that Rohit had joined them after Srivastava left so that there were three of them now. Because of his long-standing emotional attachment to village, Rohit was easy going and open hearted. But even Rohit failed to appreciate their prolonged stay in the rural town of Patharagara. All the work schedules were the same; one hardly distinguishable from the other. Couldn't all the forms have been filled, sitting at the district headquarters? It's the cynical men and women of the world that were the real problem; they refused to concede they were in the wrong if they came across a situation contrary to their expectations!

Pathargara was a rather undistinguished village. There was nothing there like you see in the Hindi movies – no cunning, ambitious farmers or their henchmen. The land distribution had been fairly equitable. One couldn't cook up an inflated account for the sake of a report. There was a separate well for the lower castes which they resented. In actual fact even the few households of the Munda Adivasis refused to allow the Harijans to touch their food. Ruku was struck by the presence of intolerance among those she had expected to be bound by common interest, namely the Dalits. The primary and the middle schools of Pathargara were situated alongside, an empty field with a fig tree standing in its midst. The boundary wall of the middle school building had collapsed and its tiled roof had a huge gap. The teacher and the students hardly sat inside for fear the entire building might cave in. They sat under the fig tree in the winter although the tree offered little protection from the cold. They were assembled at the veranda now that the summer heat was on.

A goat had climbed up on the verandah of the primary school; a dog slept with its nose buried in its curled tail. The soft soil of the floor was uneven due to the constant trudge of men's feet. There was only one teacher for the entire school. Two others, among the three appointed, had stopped coming long ago. One of them ran a shop in the adjoining village of Samrai; no one knew whether the other was alive. In her rounds, Ruku discovered boys and girls roaming all over the place instead of going to school. When she enquired about the reason for this their mothers told her that the teacher beat them up. Ruku was amazed. The teachers themselves looked as if they were barely alive!

The Headmaster of the middle school wouldn't let go of Ruku and her companions once they appeared. He had sent so many applications and had done so much canvassing for the school without results; the roof had not got repaired. Perhaps now something might be done. He took out mounds of papers, diagrams, maps from the termite-infested, broken-down cupboard and began to calculate the costs. If the honorable sirs could only put in a word things might get moving.

The spring had come to its end and the summer was about to begin its onslaught all over the region like some fierce tiger. The red flowers of Palash were still in bloom; its naked, knotty branches stood out against the evening sky.

The silhouette of flaming red flowers at the distance caught Ruku's eyes. It was the onset of a long period of famine! The resources of the small and the marginal farmers were rapidly dwindling. The landless labourers had already been out of work. One couldn't be too sure about April showers. If the soil was not moist enough it would be near impossible to plough the land at the beginning of July. It was also the time for a lot of mortgage transactions. The money lender could easily charge one and half rupees' interest on ten rupees. It took some time for Ruku to learn that the amount was the interest for the month and not the year. The water level of the wells was going down. Tubewells, the few of them that existed, were all situated in the Brahmin, Kayastha and Rajput localities. Two among them were not working. The Block officials were fully aware of the problem yet they remained unrepaired. The wells in the Harijan and Adivasi slums were neither brick-built nor deep. The well in the courtyard of the village headsman, not one built by the government, was now meeting the need of the community. In fifteen days time all the wells in the village would run dry, then the men would have to run to the banks of the canal, or ponds for their baths. Already there were signs of a tug of war between farmers for water for the animals. Soon they would be dredging up river beds for drinking water! Agitation over water was not yet on their agenda, there were no reports of blood baths, but Ruku knew their time had come.

Ruku was here for a few days – to observe, to collect data. She would be packing and leaving as soon as the work was done – she knew all this yet a feeling of pain kept welling up inside her. She couldn't talk about it. Her companions would brush aside her feelings and say, "Our outlook must not be one of problem solving ... why are you getting so involved?" Ruku sent out a report about the broken-down school building and the need to and restore the tubewells to a working order. Thank goodness nobody had an inkling about what she wrote!

She sat on the bed and looked at the questionnaire forms. Who had prepared them? Do they realise how she felt volunteering to ask those questions sitting on the only rickety chair of a person's house, confident she would get jaundice if she drank the water they offered. The peasants and the farm labourers think that heaven is at their door if they answer the questions. They sit folding their mud-coated palms and scout the skies with vacant eyes to give a suitable reply. Their veiled wives and naked children stand at the door and listen without interrupting

"What is your name? Your age? How much land do you possess? Does all of it belong to you alone? Twenty decimals?

How much do you earn per month? Don't know? Then per annum, as a guess? How do you manage? Do you work in farms belonging to others? Own buffaloes? (they squint their eyes and look at the floor), None! A plough? what else was left for her to ask? Is there a tubewell, a bicycle, a scooter? How much is the plinth area of your house? Is there a toilet, a cowdung gas plant?

By now Ruku had stopped asking such questions. She gave a cross against most queries after ascertaining the area of land they held and the availability or otherwise of bullocks and ploughs. Sudev and Mohini called around the Brahmin and Rajput localities. Perhaps they had a better impression of the movable and immovable properties of folks there. Sudev was extremely cunning. He would sit on the cot placed in a person's courtyard and get all the people of the locality to gather there. In this way he didn't have to go through the motions. He would place ten forms alongside and fill them up simultaneously. The enthusiastic Matric-failed youths and workers of the village panchayat were only to eager to lend him a hand. Mohini's face got flushed at this slight exertion. She looked annoyingly at Sudev and sighed heavy sighs! The next day Sudev went out all by himself, while Mohini lolled in bed and read a film-mag.

How does one get to know facts not covered in the printed questionnaire forms – like the death of Lakshman Dusad's two children soon after they were born? What did they die of? Was Lakshman able to get medicines from the the dispensary at Samrai, situated some five miles away? Who provided him with a loan before the outbreak of the monsoon? What was the rate of interest? What did Mahajan Rambilash Singh tell Lakshman before the panchayat elections? Where was the bank? How much money did the panhayat sevaks extort from him before lending him money to feed his cows?

Ruku managed to get all the information out of Lakshman only after considerable familiarity – information which was of no use to the government. But Ruku had what she was looking for. Those facts were not written down – they were etched in her soul. The sunset created rainbow waves in the sky. The air of late evening was filled with a sooty smell. Ruku slowly walked back home. Her companions had got so impatient before the work ended that they had no scruples about abandoning old-fashioned notions of chivalry and ditching her. Ruku was alone.

The open market space looked desolate; only a few bamboo poles, ropes, dried palm leaves to make thatched roofs with, lay scattered. A gust of wind suddenly lifted up dust from the human footprints. There was so much commotion, financial transactions at this very place for two days during the week; it had become so quiet now that it was night. The mud track next to the market place was lined on its either side with huge trees: *shirish*, *mahua*, mango and *arjun*. There were no slums in the vicinity. Ruku found the way home rather enchanting! The strong scent of mango blossoms seemed to mingle with the smell of the flowers of the *mahua*. The nocturnal atmosphere had turned sluggish, pressing her down amidst the latticework of light and shadow. So many thoughts, memories, not clear even to Ruku's own perceptions, came to her mind as she breathed in the heavy fragrance.

After Madhaya Pradesh was Bihar. One had to travel a long way beyond Bihar – from the west to the east – to arrive at the throbbing metropolis where evening had now come down. What does one do with four *batashas*, offered to the gods, after extinguishing the evening lamp? The mother takes one, the father another, the remaining two are stored in the sugar container. Umamashi at her covered varendah, Ma at the window, busily chatting away ... Phalgun flat out on the bed, holding a book up to his eyes, with the table lamp on. "The boy is so depressed since you left ... he used to gad about all the time, look what's happened to him now! These days he keeps himself, buried in books when at home, picks up his violin only occasionally. Remember the fuss he used to make about food? Now he sits quietly and eats whatever I give him. I worry he'll fall ill ... it's not natural for him to be so quiet," Umamashi had written.

"I can't bear to turn my eyes towards your house ... something seems to have dropped off the body of the house – my favourite colours! They are all missing, they have been wiped off. I know Mashima would be happy if I sit with her but I can't bring myself to do that, dear. I'm tired of all this loneliness, nothing makes me feel happy. At times I put on Bach and let its notes stream into your room. I look up at your window. I wonder, at times, where lies the source of joy of the creators of such magnificent melodies! What makes the birds so chirpy! I don't know whether the music reaches your ears, I still keep it on. I feel that the stream of happiness within my heart is running dry. I think of you , read what you write, but nothing seems to fill up the emptiness. I look pale. I have become thin. You were so involved with me, how could you leave me so easily? You don't need to become anyone great, Ruku, come back to me ... You won't recognize me if you are too late." Phalgun's letter had arrived the day before in the official mail. It had gone to Mussoorie and was redirected to her.

Ruku had gone off to sleep reading the letter. The light was on as Mohini took a long time to get to bed. Ruku lay with her hands shielding her eyes and dreamt terrible dreams in her half-awake state. Broken bits of dark blue and green glass were floating all about her. They suffocated her, as she lay enclosed by them in an atmosphere devoid of air or light. By the morning all that was forgotten and she remembered how she had stood in the *mahua* scent-filled darkness the previous night. Her heart ached as if it were about to burst.

In reality Ruku had two sides to her personality: she was both one and the other. She continually observed with detachment the suffering of that part of herself she had left behind in Calcutta. She felt she was a tree whose roots lay in Phalgun's world and its branches soared high in the flaming evening sky overhead. How was it that she had simply come away leaving him behind? But was it really that simple? She felt a bit angry with herself. Didn't she cry the day she was leaving and say she didn't want to go, didn't she beg to stay back? Umamashi, Kaku ... every one made such a fuss and came after her. Phalgun was hopping mad. "How can you let go such an opportunity!" A cab was called and before she knew she was rushed to the Howrah Station. Rain pelted down on the tin roof of the platform. Soon the train pulled out and melted into the distance amidst rain and smog; she was hardly aware what had happened. There was no one next to her. What could she do? Now Phalgun accused her of abandoning him as if she were to be blamed for everything!

"Those who stay on, those ... their universe remains unchanged and they feel the pain of separation anew each day. It is they who must undergo the trial by fire. But those who go far away enjoy relative peace, as for them the world is continually made afresh and there is no small comfort in being able to see life in an altered perspective:" Phalgun's opening sentences – in the letter he had written.

Phalgun haggard and pale? She found that hard to believe! There was always so much joy within him – he would get hold of new books each day, sing, buy new records, go after her. But there was a single source of inspiration behind it all. Once that dried up Phalgun felt bereft, as if the light had gone out. He was like a huge moth with singed wings groping from one end of the wall to the other.

"Come back again ... taking the gulmohar swept road of Spring, the road you took ere you left. Let your beauty, like the lotus flower at dawn, unfold its splendour in front of my wonder-struck eyes! I don't know anyone but you – haven't since I opened my eyes to the world around me." Phalgun, of course, never said anything of the kind. How could a childhood friend use those words? But Ruku could sense them glittering brightly in his opaque silence. Who but Ruku could?

"No, Phalgun, you must not languish in my absence. Your fragrance, your song can never fade away! You are my childhood. You have helped me to discover myself like the lamp that sheds light to illuminate the dark. I will go back to you, taking some other vibrant road if the gulmohar covered path is forever closed to me. You must wait for me –mustn't go away!"

Ruku became conscious that tears were streaming uncontrolled from her eyes as she stood under the shade of the strange oak tree of Pathargara. They glistened on the fine net of her *chunni* like drops of dew. She realised she had to get back. The village was close by and the lights had begun to appear. A hazak' lamp glowed on the verandah of Bharat Prasad's house. Akhlu Singh's back door, his cow shed and the kitchen came next. Ruku walked on spiritless as if she was a robot. All of a sudden something stirred in the dark. The smell of dust and perspiration assaulted her nose. Lachhmi rushed out, crying "Didi," in a feeble voice. Why was the girl here at this hour?

"I was waiting for you ... they won't let me talk in the house – my husband, my mother and father-in-law. You'll be going away tomorrow and I won't see you again. I feel so sad!" Her eyes, her nose ring and ear tops, were glistening in the dark; there were no tears in her eyes.

"Come, Lachhmi, let's go home," Ruku pulled her by the shoulders but Lachhmi refused to budge and stood sullenly like an obstinate mule.

"It's been six years now since the day I got married. I lost a girl child and I can't get pregnant any more. My husband beats me, day in and day out. Do you know how many gashes there are on my back, my neck and shoulders? All these days he was quiet; he controlled himself because all of you were here. He didn't beat me up. I know he will start beating me again – from tomorrow. "The sahibs and magistrates have gone, who's there to protect you?" he'll say. I don't have parents; my brother hardly comes. How can I go to my parent's home unescorted? I wish he wouldn't torture me like this every day but kill me off once for all. Will you take me with you? I can do everything – cook, clean, milk the cows. I won't be a nuisance ... I'll stay with you."

That Dinesh, such a big coward, he hid under the bed when Mansoor so much as cleared his throat! And he's given to wife-bashing? Dinesh doesn't have to fear retaliation hitting out at her. Ruku stared at the luminous dot on Lachhmi's forehead. The bun of her hair was knotty and dark.

One could call up the Superintendent of the police straightaway, Ruku thought, and his men would come and interrogate Dinesh. But if Dinesh were to give his wife a bad name and turn her out into the street would the Pathargara community come to her aid? Her brother won't let her into his house; her near ones won't take her in. The sneak! Ruku felt nothing but utter contempt for Dinesh's timidity but couldn't decide what to say to him. The law of the land can within a moment break up a family. Was there a place in this society to provide shelter for a married woman?

Anurag Srivastava would, no doubt, remark "What's the point in worrying about Lachhmi. How many Lachhmis can you take care of?" But if she can't rescue all of them must she not try to save at least one person, Ruku argued within herself. Nevertheless, without saying anything further, she caught hold of Lachhmi's sweaty hand and led her on. "I'll talk to Dinesh ... I'll ..."

Lachhmi pulled her hand away and proceeded to her own room. Her body was still firm and she had a subdued smile on her face; the dot on her forehead glittered in the dark.

"Don't tell him anything ..." the girl interrupted. "He'll beat me to pulp if he gets to know I've talked to you. You'll have gone far in your cars by then."

Bewildered Ruku slipped into her room and immediately noticed Mohini's suitcase lying unfastened on the floor. They would be leaving Pathargara the next day and travel straight from there to the district head quarters where, after a night's stay, they must catch the train to Delhi. It was time she packed her belongings. There were so many documents! They'll will have to be made into separate packets. In her absent-minded state Ruku hadn't noticed that all other members of her team had assembled in the room – Mansoor, Rohit, Sudev and Mohini. Mansoor and Rohit were standing in silence. They looked up when Ruku came in. Mansoor held a piece of paper – a wireless meassage. "A terrible tragedy Ruku ... The police station had a message from Tikamgarh, our friend Swarup is no more!" To Ruku the crumbling walls of the room seemed to totter along with its roof. Her lips moved as if to ask what had happened. She had thought that one had to be careful on a village visit as one could easily come down with fever or get typhoid – but not this!

"He was drowned in a wild river. He wanted to swim but didn't know how to. Anurag Srivastava has left for Tikamgarh, the body must be brought back ..."

"Swarup's home is in Hoshiarpur, so far away ..." Sudev added anxiously. All of a sudden the image of New Delhi Station with Swaruplall and Sunila Oram side by side, smiling away, floated in Ruku's mind's eye. Their train was due to leave late at night, Ruku and her companions had seen them off and returned home. Sunila was making so much noise – not allowing Swarup to carry her suitcase. Swarup was adamant about taking it. "Just see, Rukmini, she won't listen to anything I tell her ... she thinks I don't have the strength to lift her bag." He had complained while a smile full of love and pity had played around Sunila's lips. Wasn't that ten days ago? And already Swarup's spirit was being wafted away by the mountain breeze beyond the wild basil forests!

Anurag Srivastava had tried to dissuade her at first in gentle English, then by mixing Hindi and English words and finally in angry Hindi. Actually the person was no more, they were merely carrying a corpse. Where was the need for her to accompany them? He was taking the dead body along with him, Naresh Mathur was joining him at Delhi. Besides girls shouldn't get involved in the matter at all. In India no girls accompany the dead. But Sunila would hear none of it.

She had sat quietly, her hair bun intact, although she hadn't run a comb through her hair since the day before – hadn't broken down with grief. The body had arrived the previous evening after much effort made by the people in the district. Anurag Srivastava had planned to return to Delhi after his field visits. He had to stay back receiving the news. An extra coach was being attached to the train leaving for Delhi by special request from the National Academy. A glass-enclosed van was to be kept waiting in Jullunder. Anurag had arranged for everything with extraordinary promptness. A few colleagues lost their sleep at the other end of the line. The Home minister didn't dilly-dally but got in touch post haste with the airports of Madhaya Pradesh, Punjab and Delhi through official channels. Where was Sunila's place in all this? In fact in his innermost thoughts, Anurag couldn't forgive her.

The boy didn't know how to swim. Why did he have to go into the river? Did the girl play a role instigating him? These boys and girls who came on village visits and formed into groups with their dear friends ... were the unsurveyed backward villages a place to make love? Was Swarup trying to impress his beloved? The other three in their team were nowhere around. And what happened to the social code of conduct – where to go and where not to go – that he had drilled into their heads during his briefing? Now Sunila goes on repeating she wants to see his mother, just this once! Does this emotion have any meaning? Anurag failed to dissuade her even after several trys. Sunila had got into the car quietly sending off her luggage and her friends. Now a dull and tough journey lay ahead for her.

Swarup's country, his home, was so far away. There were no addresses or directions to get to the place but one had to reach there, no matter how. A heavy blue curtain had come down in front of Sunila's eyes as, the train speeded through rice fields on a russet afternoon – the sky was deep blue edged by forests of different shades of green. It was past mid day. The two of them had walked away from the camp; there were five others in the inspection bungalow. Kuldeep had been cooking chicken, romping all over the place making war cries! ah! ah! Suraj the chawkidar was fed up with all his advice and demands. The five of them were due to leave the place the day after. Suraj had already succeeded in acquiring two old shirts, Sunila's old saree for his wife and was tying them into a bundle. Seeing Swarup going out, Kuldeep had shouted, "Ei, get back soon. I won't wait if I feel hungry."

Sunila had smiled. Everyone knew Kuldeep would keep on sitting, knees folded and read a book if any one of the group was late in getting back but he always shouted at others to sit down and eat. Last night, tired settling his suitcase, Kuldeep had danced all over the room, holding a big old umbrella and singing the well-known song from the film 420 – *"Pyar hua, ikrar hua, pyar se kiu darta hai dil!"* How could one help loving Kuldeep whose sparkling almond coloured eyes exuded so much innocent fun? Had anyone else danced, one would have thought him loutish and crude.

Walking away from the woods bordering the village Swarup and Sunila had reached a running stream. They had come here a few times earlier, during late afternoons. The little stream ran along the edge of a sandbank and took a bend at a distance. There were sparse woods on its either side. It was a hushed afternoon interrupted only by sounds of sweet twittering from the nearby trees.

"Ei, what's happening with you?" Sunila placed her hand on Swarup's shoulders. They were sitting on the dry portion of the river bank. "You've become so quiet since yesterday."

"It's nothing, really, "Swarup tried to smile.

"You're hiding something ... from me. Are you homesick??"

Swarup didn't utter a word in response. The river flowed soundlessly in front of them. An empty clay pitcher lay abandoned. Perhaps someone had come from the village to fetch water. Swarup hadn't been able to send any money home for the past three months. All his money had been spent on food and sundry items in this place. Other boys had money sent from home. In his case the question didn't rise. How could his father help him out when he himself, had to borrow in order to pay off interest on loan? Lord knew what his mother thought about him ... she must imagine that her son was earning thousands of rupees and wasn't sending her any. She had probably hoped their situation would change drastically once the son had a job, the girls would have good marriage offers and all the people in the village would share their happiness. But that had not been possible.

The two had sat a long time on the river bank the previous evening – Swarup's head on Sunita's lap, Sunila's fingers softly caressing his hair. Swarup had given his word he would opt for Bihar so that Sunila was not put under a great strain. Her father had become paralyzed after a stroke and Sunila couldn't think of leaving him and going elsewhere. But suppose she had to ... what then? No, in that case she would prefer to remain a virgin the rest of her life, Sunila had made up her mind.

"And what if we are compelled to stay apart after marriage?" Swarup had asked.

The distance between the Punjab and Bihar was meaninglessly vast. What was the sense in getting married if the two were made to stay so far apart from each other? It was better to remain friends. Swarup could guess from all the letters she wrote, her phone calls, even the way she smiled that the thought was causing her a deep anguish.

"Doesn't matter, I'll come to your region ... how'd you like that? "At once Sunila tugged at his soft hair and gave him a dimpled smile.

But Swarup had felt terribly burdened at the thought of living up to his promise. Why was that. Was he unhappy because he would be going so far away from his mother and sisters? Sunila had been ambling light-heartedly, like some yellow-beaked singing blackbird, ahead of him How could she fathom Swarup's wounded feelings?

Swarup had walked back to his camp in great haste without glancing back. He had felt a noose tightening around his neck. He worried that he was incapable of taking it off. Sunila was chatting away with Kuldeep at the dinner table, squabbling with him in jest. She was badgering innocent Ramphal Singh by hiding his chappals ... how could she suspect Swarup's feeling of a sudden loss?

"Are you homesick?" Sunila gave his shoulders another push. Sarup got up gazing at the obscure forest around the river bend. He smiled and stretched out his arms.

"I'm hot, I want to take a swim ... you go and sit behind the trees."

"It's not necessary, I'm shutting my eyes," "she closed her eyes and stuck out her tongue, "Issh."

"Go there, I'm telling you ... it's alright now, sit back to the front." Sunila had walked some distance and sat under a tree facing the opposite direction. It would have been nice to have had a book to read now, she thought. Swarup took his trousers and shirt off and entered the water with his pants.

It was noon yet the water was hardly warm. It was bound to get much colder by the evening. Swarup felt wonderful. Daylight dazzled his eyes – the mild water lapped around his knees, it rose slowly upto his waist – the song of the blackbirds rang in his ears and entered his soul. He had swum in the university pool when he was a student. Coming to the river bend he tried to dive into the water. The river there was so deep that it seemed to have no bottom. Within minutes Sarup's handsome but diffident form was engulfed by the swirling waves; a lifeless figure was caught up by an ancient babla tree in the depths. Swarup had imagined the veranda of his small dilapidated house that rubbed against a world of wild woods – there, the crows sat feasting on the stale bread and his youngest barely-teethed baby sister sat displaying her most enchanting smile. A mere child, she had put her wet arms around his neck – what strength her tender arms had – all this before he finally lost consciousness.

"Swarup ..." Sunila called out impatiently, coming out from behind the trees. What a long time the boy was taking to bathe! The water was calm, the woods awesome, the birds ... nothing echoed back.

Swarup had been absent minded for some days. He had been suffering from a nervous debility long before the incident had taken place It was quite out of character for him to swim in the river, not giving a thought, especially because he had no experience of rivers. Sunila should have had some sense, not sat by herself such a long time without showing any concern. Actually Sunila had had her own hesitations about preventing him from swimming in the river. Suppose he had thought she wanted to curb his freedom? She was at peace with herself knowing that Swarup had at last accepted her with his whole being. But somewhere something had seemed wrong.

And she remembered her discomfiture at the images of his veiled mother, his farmer father, and his three sisters in the black-white photograph, taken by some moffusil photographer, Swarup always carried. Never mind, hadn't Sunila been honoured by the great sacrifice he was about to make in relation to his family? Sunila had felt she must follow him without a murmur and not contradict him in anyway.

Sitting under the tree her thoughts had wandered back to the red gravelled road that ran upto her house in Ranchi. Red bougenvillia plants covered its roof. She must bring Swarup to her father. Both of them must go to see him in pride and joy; she musn't visit her father by herself. Baba had been so unhappy about Sunila's leaving home. She must make a joke of it now and make her father happy.

A devastated Sunila caught a glimpse of Kuldeep as soon as the train entered the Delhi Station.

"What's this, you didn't go back?" She asked.

"I was ... I changed my mind mid-journey. You are travelling so far all alone. It's a place I know, have many acquaintances there, many contacts ... don't worry."

Kuldeep wouldn't listen to any of her objections. He sat by her side and showered her with sympathy and affection, making Anurag Srivastav more annoyed. Kuldeep rushed to bring her coffee at the airport, carried her suitcase all over the place, made all the necessary phone calls.

A small Foker Friendship plane flew between Delhi and Jullunder. It didn't fly high but made enough noise to burst the ear drums. Sunila sat resting her aching shoulders on the high back of the aeroplane seat. She looked out at the view of the sky. Bright white rays of dawn were peeping through the minarets of clouds. Sunila had never observed such a sight! It was her first time on a plane yet she didn't feel the joy of flying. The plane was carrying a wooden cask with Sarup's body in its inner compartment. It glided over the dry, rolling wheat fields; there was no water to be seen, or any reflection of sunlight on water after they crossed the river Jamuna. Sunila's life had taken such a dramatic turn in the past twenty four hours! Yesterday she and Swarup had been walking towards the river – the sky was such a deep blue, her eyes had feasted on an ensemble of so many different colours, she had heard the twittering sound of different parakeets – today there was nothing.

Decades later when Sunila's life had dried up and cast aside like some sun singed *amloki* fruit from the tree, the retired Commissioner of Ranchi, Sunila Oram was, suddenly trembled while she sat and hastily shut the book she held on her lap. She tousled the unruly locks of white hair which fell on her forehead and closed her eyes. She had seen through the faint beam of light at the end of a long tunnel, how the village people had crowded around the glass enclosed van carrying Swarup's dead body; how his mother had gone for Kuldeep like a fierce tigress after a few moments of stunned silence. Her nails and bangles had left scratches all over Kuldeep's face. No one noticed Sunila, no one had spoken to her.

Anurag Srivastav had held his white handkerchief to his eyes and managed the situation, speaking a mixture of Hindi and English words in a hoarse voice. He hadn't forgotten to mention there was compensation due to the family for the tragedy that had ocurred. On the way back Anurag had lost no time in buying woollen clothes for his wife and children. He kept those inside the car so that no one would get to know about it. Sunila felt that the beam of light now reflecting peace and quiet within her had increased in volume and had finally wiped off the memory of that face of Swarup's mother – full of fear and violence.

Sunila's old white house has a big hall with an old fashioned fire palace in the front. Ranchi is usually very cold during the months of November and December. The veranda and the dining the room lie adjacent to the hall. One can see the lawn and the blue mountain range skirting the town from the rear window. Sunila's bedroom is to the right. The mahagony bed is draped with a lace bedcover. No one save Sunila enters the place. A framed photograph of a twenty-five-year old youth is kept on the side table; a white rose adorns the tall, metallic vase all the year around. There's also a wooden box containing ashes collected from the Hoshiarpur burning ghat that Kuldeep had given Sunila. Kuldeep too was dead – shot one morning in 1985 by terrorists. Religion was of a little use for a Sikh boy with such fund of love and sympathy and above all an innocent heart!

Sunila can hear the leaves falling in the evening's silence, she can listen to the sound of meteors landing in the dark. Life's spirit – suffused with memories and unconscious recollections – linger about her like the smell of eucalyptus leaves, long after the trees have shed them. Those days – of sun and air and love, of hazy green colours and whirring of birds – they protect Sunila; create a ring around her like a fortress and keep her safe. Life's sorrows don't touch her.

Four

One by one the buses from Delhi reached Mussoorie, holding out against the pelting rain, chilly wind and an overcast sky. Trainees who had parted from their teams arrived from Dehradoon in hired taxis; most of them had taken the night train from Delhi. The roar of the bus engine, human voices, noise of coolies running helter-skelter, and the shouts of the room bearers enlivened the atmosphere in front of the little post office. Hardly any one had an umbrella or a waterproof but Murgeshan from Tamilnadu was quite different. Cautious and finicky, he took out his shiny umbrella from its celophane wrap and slowly walked towards his Block; he was not inclined to share his umbrella with anyone. The rest reached their rooms either slightly wet or totally drenched and were clamouring for their evening tea. Thank goodness, they didn't have to attend any classes that day! Agamchand went on dishing out cups of ginger tea and *suji* biscuits to the ladies in their rooms. He was so happy to find them back after a fortnight's absence. He behaved as if he were their guardian – he alone knew the ropes.

In normal times, the lounge would get crowded before dinner with boys and girls returning from their treks or field trips. They always had so much to tell each other; they would talk noisely, laugh loudly, make a row. The atmosphere was like that of the day schools go back after the pujas or the summer holidays. Cigarettes and chewing gum in Ramlal's shop would vanish in no time. Today the boys and girls came back to a different situation. The lounge looked like a desolate market place. The few who sat there huddled together, talked in hushed tones. Many sat all by themselves with faces buried in magazines or newspapers. It was seven fifteen. Not many people had assembled there although dinner was usually served by a seven-thirty. Ramlall was not playing his music.

Peace of the campus had been shattered by a stormy event while they were away: the full enormity of the situation struck everyone like a bolt of lightning only now. In a matter of seconds feelings of anger, regret and blame peaked among the inhabitants of the mountains. Sankaran had resigned! He had sent off his letter of resignation to the Headquarters that very day, had moved out of his office room and was now in his little cottage, quietly packing away the few things he possessed. He would probably go back to the little mofussil town where he had his ancstral home. Sankaran had never been attracted by a the charms of cosmopolitan life. It wouldn't be difficult for him to return to land farming at his village in Kerala.

The boys and girls of the Academy were totally oblivious of the quick turn of events. How could they catch up with all the happenings when they were miles away? Ruku and her team in a remote village in the heart of Madhaya Pradesh, others scattered all over western UP, some at the other end of Madhaya Pradesh. They had stepped into the dream-like world of chirruping crickets, far, far beyond mainstream life, into a land without newspapers or the television. But that dream world was also not one of unalloyed happiness. It was a place where the plough lay abandoned on the unsown fields, where mud-cloaked buffaloes had wooden drums tied around their necks and where there were ragged men and women, huge *sal* trees, darkness and dispensaries without medicines ...

When Ruku rang home her father exclaimed in amazement, "What kind of people are the lot of you ... the whole world knows about it and you don't!" The incident had actually taken place at a Uttar Pradesh camp, on the fourth day of the their field trip. The protagonist was some Suresh Prasad: a product of a rich distillation of landowning class and westernised education. He had terrorised everyone even while he was at Mussoorie; no one had wished to cross his path, especially after a few unpleasant encounters. He made others lives hell with the sarcasm and rudeness. His views about women were unprintable! He was drunk most evenings. Because he refused to go to the dining hall meals had to be served in his room. As the nephew of a powerful politician and the son of an important leader of the ruling party of Uttar Pradesh, Suresh Prasad had more than one prop.

Suresh was furious that Gouri, a girl from the South, had been appointed the leader of his group. How could girls manage teams, he grumbled to himself as he got pulled up by the faculty supervisor for his taunts. A cold war had ensued between the two even before they left for their camp. Suresh refused to submit to Gauri's authority. "No, I won't have breakfast now, I'm not hungry", "You go for your field work. I'll stay back at the inspection bungalow" and "who eats all this rubbish ... for dinner?" He would smash the plate on the floor. Finally one day past midnight, when the blaring music from his stereo made the tired girls and boys desparate for sleep and when objection raised by some of them didn't work Gauri barged into his room. She had had enough! She had her night gown on; she had no choice but to come out of her room as she was.

The light in Suresh Prasad's room was on. He was listening to music, lying half-reclined on the bed. His room mate, Prithviraj, was shielding his eyes with a magazine trying to go to sleep. A bottle, a glass half-full, lay on the table. Gauri switched off the stereo without a word. It made Suresh jump up. He asked, "What the hell is the matter?"

"I have had to bring this thing to a stop ... nobody can sleep. I'll have to confiscate the machine if you put the stereo on again. Suresh gave her a dirty, cold look. Prithiviraj had gone off to sleep, he didn't stir. Gauri started to pull the plug out from the loose switch board without noticing anything.

Suresh always carried a loaded Italian pistol in one of the pockets (a fact that came to light only during investigation). He now pushed an absent-minded Gauri against the wall and pressed the pistol muzzle against her temple.

"The bullett will go right through your skull if you don't get off my back, you *badmash*!" He sounded so cool! Gauri was scared. She shut her eyes and broke out in a cold sweat; she didn't make a sound. She felt she had already left this world so sure she was she would die. Suresh didn't give up or let her go. He led her on step by step towards her own room, at gun point. It was almost one in the morning. The village was deserted; a few dogs barked in the dark. The bungalow was, in any case, far away from any human habitation. Massive trees closed in on all sides. The sudden hooting of the night owl and the chirrup from the crickets breached the silence of the night. "I'll kill you ... if you so much as open your mouth or if any one comes to know about this. I'll get rid of your body so that no one will find out." He spoke barely audibly. Gauri wouldn't have believed that a man who normally shouted like a barbarian and who threatened to beat up any person who crossed his path was capable of lowering his voice – thus. She stood clenching her teeth while all her sensibilities converged on the one milimetre spot of her forehead pressed down by the revolver muzzle.

Suresh was drunk. He could easily slip up and a bullett would pierce Gauri's skull through and through. Her back was pressed against the discoloured, crumbling wall of the hall, a dining room only by name. The room had got spruced up and the cobwebs brushed away only because the sahibs had arrived. There was no table in the hall – nothing save a rickety string cot. Dogs slept on the veranda of the dilapidated inspection bangalow most of the time. Gauri and Shirin's room was at one end of the hall; the four boys stayed at a room at the opposite end. With her back pushed against the wall, Gauri heard the faint click of a door being unlatched. A person came out wearing pyjamas; his sleepy eyes opened wide in amazement. It was Navroj! He couldn't guess what Suresh held in his grip. He saw perspiration break out on Gauri's terror-stricken face. Suresh's face was too close to hers for comfort; Navroj realised he was not witnessing a love scene.

He grabbed Suresh's waist with the swiftness of a snowbound leopard and quietly flung him on the floor in just three seconds; he took a few extra seconds to unload the revolver. Suresh lay on the floor for a moment then jumped up and sat uttering a volley of abuse in English.

Gauri had gone into her room and locked herself in. She switched the light on and held Navroj's hand in a tight grip. Her palms were cold and sweaty.

Shirin was awake; she looked bewildered and sad. Navroj meant to give her a reassuring smile when there were sounds of hard kicks against the door. His eyes blazed in anger; he was ready for a fight. He pulled his hand away from Gauri's grasp so that he could give the kick he had so far withheld.

When Navroj dragged Suresh's body like a potato-sack to

his bed and wiped off the blood stains with Suresh's own handkerchief he realised that he had given him too hard a blow. The copper ring given by his aunt Navroj had on his finger, with the engraving of Vaisno Devi, had cut into the drunkard's lips. He had to wash all the blood off.

The next day before 11 a.m. Gauri's long wireless message reached Delhi and then Mussoorrie. Suresh Prasad must be sent packing immediately! The report that Sankaran had sent to the higher ups, based on both faculty supervisor Alokranjan's investigations and a conversation with Gauri on the telephone, didn't cut any ice with the authorities. Like the arrow that overshot its mark it rebounded back on him. "How could one turn a young boy out of the academy for something he may have done in an inebriated state. He is really sorry now. Sankaran ought to behave like the Director of a National Academy and not some hostel warden." A pedictable fall out, that. Rumours began to circulate in the corridors of Delhi and the cloud immersed slopes of Mussoorie that it was not easy to dismiss a person so hightly connected as Suresh Prasad.

"Then let the inevitable happen. Suresh's crime is a cognisable and non-bailable offence in Indian Penal code; it is a case for the police yet the officer in charge is not courageous enough to come forward and book him. Suresh is a trainee officer, his permanent status in service is still an open question. I'll have to resign since no action has been taken against him in spite of all my petitions."

Sankaran himself explained the gist of the fax he had sent to the Ministry, to the faculty members at a meeting in the simplest possible words. His colleagues were stunned, as if struck by a lightning. No one stirred. Chandan Mitra from Calcutta spoke out after a while, "But suppose people interpret your resignation as cowardice – think you're escaping all the trouble?"

"Let them ... no, they won't do that. They would know I haven't fled the scene out of fear but have struck a death blow to the system. If I had bowed my head now it would have meant moral victory for them. No officer would then go after someone who is highly connected, not those who want to hang on to their jobs."

"I keep wondering how a speciman like Suresh managed to enter the academy hoodwinking the interview board," Shyamananda Sinha commented gently.

"Easy," Sankaran displayed the calculation sheet. "Suresh did well in his written exams; at the interview his proficiency in English got him more than half way there. Besides, what can an half hour interview reveal? Can it expose his hidden instincts, the criminal propensities beneath the veneer of language and manners? An educated boy may not be aware of the difference between holding knives and forks straight and showing respect to a woman colleague. When I came here I wanted to tear off the mask of politeness and civilized behaviour and uncover the real human being that exists beneath all social pretence. I have failed. The son of an illiterate herdsman Navroj, may not be aware of the niceties of social manners but he has a sound sense of human worth. As for the interview board – they wouldn't only, till the other day, tolerate regional language when spoken – wouldn't they have failed Navroj and given eighty per cent marks to Suresh?What do you have to say to that Shyamakanta?"

Ruku had felt lonely after Sankaran left. She missed the shelter of his quiet home and his warm personality. He was a person she could go to whenever she wanted, without any prior appointment: to solve a problem to rid her mind of all kind of doubts. He never dismissed any problem, as irrelevant, unreal or 'emotional'. Ruku felt his absence a hundred fold in the alien environment she found herself in. Nature played pranks constantly. It was cloudy one day, sunny the next; chilly winds and unexpected rains hardly made her feel happy. She panicked about all the things she had to fit in between now and dinner time. Where was the opportunity for her to sit quietly by herself and allow her mind to drift? The mast that stood on the ocean for the little bird to rest on had disappeared – what will the little bird now do?

Ruku had had enough of life in a golden cage, it held no charm for her. She felt cramped. A large sunfilled tree spreading its branches seemed to be calling out to her from a distance, beckoning her to return home – to the world of toiling men, energized by forces of nature. When the urge became irresistable she started packing, but that feeling subsided after a couple of days. She was seen coming out of the little post office where she had gone to make a call home – swathed in pale moonlight. She had talked to her dear ones and postponed her journey home, indefinitely. She could get through to Phalgun only once in a while, in the three to six minute call she usually made home. But that endearing prospect awaited her if she sent a message ahead. Not many words were exchanged, she heard him laugh, caught some of his words: "What ... are you writing? Yes, I'm well ... send a long letter." The operater's hoarse voice, "six minutes over ... call over," would descend like an iron crate over their heads and put an end to their conversation.

All of a sudden Ruku recalled reading English newspapers, sitting in the library's glass-encased Reading room one Sunday afternoon. She had seen Sankaran as soon as she raised her eyes. He indicated to her not to get up and said, "I read your poem in the House journal. The flavour of the original is most certainly lost in the translation, but the editor has placed the original in *devnagri* script by its side. I was able to make some sense of the poem. You have compassion, Ruku, there's nothing false about your feelings. That is your strength although many people will persuade you to the contrary. You'll have to cope with much circumstantial pressure ... effort will be made to mould you into a person you are not." Looking at clouds moving away from the green valley Sankaran said, his voice wet with tears. "But you must't abandon poetry, you musn't!"

But what if poetry abandoned her? She had heard its receding footsteps as if it were already deserting her – leaving her soul for the milder air of the higher regions – like the moon floating away, sparkling brightly ...

Had she, Ruku, become a different person, a someone else? There was an old, tarnished wooden mirror in the bathroom, where she could see the outline of her face. She saw how her face had got rounded in the few months. There was a pink glow on her cheeks: the pale drawn look of her Calcutta days had all but gone. Now her eyes were no longer dreamy but keen and alert. Her voice had acquired a tone of confidence: she could be assertive when she faced contrary arguments. Ruku hadn't possessed these qualities before. She had felt hurt time and again by the rude, selfish behaviour of boys and girls, tearing apart their mask of politeness. She had hid herself in the toilet and cried her heart out thinking about the high-pitched tone of Madhu Singh's voice or the fixed stare of Akhilesh Sharma at the breakfast table. Drops of tears had fallen and seeped through the open pages of Bibhutibhusan's Collected Works, that lay in front of her. Now Ruku was adept in tackling all kinds of situations; she remained silent or gave a sharp rejoinder as and when the situation demanded.

The person who had been at the center of Ruku's existence had abided in such a lofty place; it had been impossible for her to see him more than once or twice a month. But he had been her mentor. Sankaran knew like the palm of his hand the gap between politics of state and human beings struggling for survival – the hazy contours of that scarred landscape remained constantly in his mind's eye. He entertained no illusions about his role but didn't, therefore, understimate his power or his authority. He would say, "In no other county in this world do you have a system where administrators do their jobs living so close to the ordinary people and at the same time maintain such a distance from them. Be true to yourself and give your best. Remember always for whose interest you work. Neutrality has no meaning in matters of administration. You are a total failure if you have no commitment towards the underpriviledged or the marginalized."His voice would sink into a whisper.

"In actual fact all this talk about committed bureaucracy is hogwash, as fake as 'a golden bowl made out of stoneware', There's no such concept in theory." Atish Jha, a former leader of JNU student's union, declared sticking his fork into Ramesh's *parathas*. Sankaran had already gone and Atish was rapidly arriving at his own conclusions, altering his previously held stance. With Sankaran no longer there to contradict him, he didn't feel the need to hold on to an idea which had no theoretical validity for him. Privately he hadn't got over the blow Sankaran had given him before he left.

Atish had sent Sankaran a card with the words: "We are with you in your fight", written in red ink and signed "a well wisher". Atish didn't give his name: he was worried the card might get misplaced and he would be taken to task if it got into other people's hands. Atish was astonished by Sankaran's reaction. Not only had he recognized his handwriting but had sent the card back accompanied by a short note: "Write when you have the courage to reveal your identity, not before." Atish was crushed; he swallowed the humiliation in silence but didn't forget about it.

On the face of it, Sankaran's departure at that particular junecture made him breathe more easily: he was about to get engaged to the daughter of the DIG of Jashimabad Range. He would've been really embarassed if that news had reached

Sankaran's ears. There was nothing unusual about the proposed union save the fact Atish had settled for "kinds" instead of "cash,"as dowry. It could not have remained a secret for long. Former revolutionary Atish didn't lack enemies. The sum of eight lack of rupees was actually peanuts in today's world. Boys like Ram Mishra and Rajkamal hadn't settled for anything less than thirty or thirty five! Ram had demanded two cars instead of one in two different models, Rajkamal two sets of furniture, TV and Fridge, so that one of them could be given to his sister on her marriage. The boys belonging to the first-year class were so worldly: they understood bank balance, interest, share index and such matters. Atish had had to undergo much harassment over his sister's wedding. His sister was such a beauty, a first class in Msc, yet there was no end of trouble trying to fix her up with the son of his mother's childhood friend.

It hardly made a difference that the boy had yet to complete his medical studies or that he had frequently come to their home and Atish's mother had fed him sumptuous meals. Forcing a faint smile Dipak had told him to his face, "We must postpone the matter for now, *Bhaiya*, I'm all alone, how many parties can I negotiate with, at the same time? I'm screening the applications. I'll start talks with those who are willing to deposit a lakh and half to my account, book a car for me in advance ... I'll return the money if negotiations fail. It'll take atleast a fortnight to complete these formalities. We can have a round of discussion then, what do you think?" Swallowing the insult, an angry Atish had returned home. He had to sell off his mother's ornaments; the ancestral land in Bihar Sharif hadn't added up to much. Friends in Mussoorie had commented: "Is anything wrong if a girl remains unmarried?" How would people from the South or Bengal know what happened to a girl if she wasn't married off in the North? Atish had also managed to recover the financial commitments he had to make for his sister's marriage by manipulating his own. He had been able to get the better of his defeat.

Ruku was returning to her room, hugging the excercise books she had bought when she came across Navroj, at the gate. He had just got back from the town.

Navroj hadn't revealed anything about the incident involving Suresh Prasad to anyone; not even to Ruku. She had got to know about it from none other than Gauri herself. She couldn't stop congratulating Navroj for the heroic role he had played. Navroj hung his head and looked the other way, feeling shy and awkward. A month had gone by, everyone was upset over Sankaran's leaving and the history behind Navroj's bravery was all but forgotten. Ruku and Navroj had come face to face after a long time today. Navroj had been avoiding her – it wasn't difficult for Ruku to understand why. She herself was not inclined to brush aside the embarassment one felt after such an experience. Navroj couldn't forget what had taken place the night before Ruku left for her field trip, although he had kept on trying. Ruku, too, had done her best to erase the memory of that evening from her mind. She had understood that she had to overcome what she couldn't forget, otherwise she would never feel free.

"Come ... let's sit for a while, shall we?" Ruku began.

Far away the company gardens had disappeared behind the rolling mists. A candle burned in Ramesh's shop and the sodium lights in the streets had dimmed into a mauvish haze. Suddenly there was an electricity failure. Ruku and Navroj had to return to the canteen. There wasn't a sound about the place, no one was there – Ramesh, his wife or his mother. They sat facing eath other at the bare table. Navroj spoke after some moment's silence, "Have you written to Sonal?"

"Yes, why do you ask?" There was a note of amusement in Ruku's voice.

"Did you get a reply? Won't you show it to me?"

"Why should I? The letter is *my* property now!"

Ruku didn't tell Navroj that Sonal had sent a photograph of herself along with the letter. A mass of black hair with a thin middle parting. Her two thick plaits fell on the either side of her shoulders. She had eyes like those of a fawn, big, filled with awe and tenderness. Her nose was rather sharp, lips thin. Although Ruku couldn't guess at her complexion from that black and while photograph, she had no doubt at all the girl belonged to the snow-clad hills. The words "your Sonal," was scribbled at the back of the picture. Sonal had completely missed out the two consonants in the middle of Rukmini's name and had substituted an 'h' in its place.

Sonal's letter, written in big scrawl, was filled up with stories about her mother – a widow – who worked with the panchayat so that she could earn enough to support her family. Sonal had written about her village and also about Navroj. She hadn't mentioned him by name but referred to him indirectly like married women did in the country. She had written that their bethrothal ceremony couldn't take place because of Navroj's problems. He used to visit them all the time when he lived in the neighbourhood. Now he was so far away ... she hadn't seen him for such a long time! Ruku felt as if a gush of air carrying the smell of Phulpur had suddenly blown in from across the borders of Jammu.

The Jwaladevi temple was situated near the border. From the Phulpur railway station Sonal could see the Himalayas spread against the sky while smoke rolled out of the walls and the floors of Jwaladevi's cave. For the religious minded the smoke had different names and different explanations. Sonal and Navroj loved to sit on a bench at the station platform and play a game of make-believe travelling. At the end of the platform shed lay a sprawling ground of concrete, surrounded by deserted fields. The dark blue mountains rose steeply at a distance, their primeval appearance sent waves of wonder among the dumb-founded people.

Navroj had never told Ruku anything about the extent of humiliation Sonal and her mother had had to endure. It was Kuldeep who had. Sonal's mother was the widow of a Brahmin yet she had been compelled to take up the job of a *gram sevika* for money. She took care of the accounts, distributed seeds, arranged the midwife's visit if a woman was in labour. She had to walk to three or four villages during summer, winter and the monsoon season. There were no buses by which she could travel to distant places, she had no safeguards whatsoever – neverthless she was a Brahmin's widow! A low sub-caste boy came visiting her. The boy walked beside her daughter on the main street of a neighbouring village, the audacity! The boy had the gumption to call at her house, lie on her bed – Mohanlall, the panchayat's peon had seen all this with his own eyes. The village pradhan, Raghupati Dwivedi's long fair face turned red as copper in anger. He called Sonal's Ma and said "Does society not exist just because your husband is dead? Turn the low-caste scum out of your house, else you'll have to quit work and leave the village!"

Sonal's Ma was small built and fat. She had just turned forty. Her sunburnt face had brown patches and her hair had started greying at roots. She always carried a small box of betel leaf with her and pushed a *pan* into her mouth whenever her throat felt dry. Although she trembled at Dwivedi's remark she also remembered how Navroj would rest his head on her lap when she had sat on the veranda of her house in the evenings, spreading the mattress. He would demand she fondled his hair and refused to eat unless she fed him, squeezing the boiled rice into little round balls. Poor thing, he had lost his mother when he was a child ... how he hankered for motherly love! Could she throw him out of her house just because he belonged to the lower caste? Yet, as of now, no one had an inkling only the other day he had asked for Sonal's hand. It was during an evening when he was about to leave and Sonal had been busy making the bed. Navroj had come and stood in front of her with his head bowed. Usha's heart had almost stopped beating seeing him thus. She hoped against hope he wouldn't say anything she didn't want to hear or make her feel afraid.

But Navroj did utter the fateful words. He spoke as if to himself, without lifting his head or looking up at her, "Mummy, I know I don't deserve anything ... I'm not respected in this society but if you have any compassion you'll understand ... and allow me to bring Sonal to my home."

Perhaps all kinds of prejudices, beliefs in social customs which lay dormant within her had raised their heads. She blurted out before she realised what she was saying, "Shame! shame! you bare-faced creature! How could you utter those words? Oh God, who knows who might have heard all this talk ... I will be banished from the village." Sonal's Ma turned into stone she hardly had spoken these harsh words. She was struck by the brutality of her own feelings.

Sonal came running there, broom in her hand. She saw Navroj standing quietly with tear-filled eyes.

Usha Debi was compelled to control herself. She became more tender towards him, "But there is something called social custom, dear boy. The girl's guardians have to go to the boy's father with the proposal. Would your father and uncle listen to us?"

They wouldn't, of course, nor allow the mother and daughter to step into their courtyard – didn't Navroj know that? He shook his head, "No, you don't have to tell them anything ... I'll do whatever necessary, I and my friends."

"But can a marriage ceremony be performed in this manner?

Here – the entire community will ostracise me, there – your father and uncle will point their guns at me. My girl will be thrown into an abyss. Who'll protect her if she's in danger?"

"You will, Ma and Jwaladevi ... who else do we have? Don't say no to him." The girl was right behind them holding a duster. Rukmini had filled in the bare bones of the incident Kuldeep had related to her with the help of her imagination. She had taken the story of Navroj's courtship and marriage proposal apart at the seams and rewritten the narrative in the form of several episodes. In actual fact, Navroj had indeed gone to Usha with the marriage proposal and Usha couldn't refuse him. Navroj had given her his word. That's how the matter had now stood.

But yes, Usha had quacked in her bones when she stood, head bowed, in front of Dwivedi, the panchayat's pradhan. Dwivedi had commented on Navroj's visits, his resting on her bed – if he had known that Navroj was her prospective son-in-law he would have surely exposed her, turned her out of the village. Usha remembered how Novroj looked when he lay buried in her lap – his sun bronzed forehead, his thick hair, like the green undergrowth of the river Beas – could one put down child one once takes into one's lap?

Openly, Usha had remarked,"The boy is an orphan. He's the nephew of a dear friend. He comes and sits with us. I don't have the heart to turn him out. But I'll speak to him, explain ... so that he comes less often."

"Less often!" Dwivedi had repeated the two words in anger. "Yes, we are absolutely against the idea of his visiting you.

We'll make you are a destitute if you don't show proper respect for our norms and customs. You may go now."

It had been the beginning of the mother and daughter's lonely, degraded existence. They hadn't been ostracised by the community or deprived of the ordinary amenities of life in a village but they had lived in utter shame. Young boys gave them a smirky smile at bus stops; people they knew turned away their faces or lowered their heads when they came across them in the market place. The other day, the old priest of Vishnu temple had stepped back a couple of paces while he was distributing *charanamrita*. He wanted to avoid being contaminated by them, perhaps. Usha had come home that evening and doused the kitchen fire with water; she didn't speak to Sonal. At that time Navroj was undergoing training for his new job. Letters from him came far and few. It was difficult to get leave, the pressure of work was heavy, he had written. He had gone away so far from them! The mother and daughter took his absence to heart. They felt sad when they took out the hot *roti* from the oven or mixed the *rajma* curry with *ghee* prepared from cow's milk. Navroj's old umbrella and a pair of chappals lay abandoned in their house: they couldn't bear to look at them.

Dark rings had begun to appear under Sonal's eyes. Her cheek bones became so prominent that the blue veins were visible. Usha noticed Sonal had become miserably thin and suddenly began to feel extremely apprehensive. She hoped nothing improper had happened; she prayed to allay her worst fears. The girl had been in her room with Navroj for long stretches of time while she worked outside. But Usha gathered her thoughts and scolded herself. How could she, a mother, think ill of her own daughter? Her heart ached at the thought and she bemoaned the fact she hadn't made enough effort to finalise the wedding although she had to put up with so much indignity. Navroj had left the village as soon as his results were out. But Sonal could not be given in marriage to any one else; the entire community knew about them. Navroj was far away, at a training college, where there were many pretty and educated girls. Suppose he had a change of heart?

Usha hadn't tried to receive the holy water from the priest. She had merely saluted him with folded palms and bowed her head against the temple wall. She had rung the temple bell. No food was cooked that night as she had already doused the oven with water. A storm rose in the early hours of the morning and dust swept by a tree-shaking wind entered their room. The mother and daughter had been lying side by side. Drops of icy rain fell over them. It was the end of winter yet there was hardly any respite from the cold. Usha had to get up to shut the window. The kitchen usually got wet when the lashing rain forced open the door. She returned to her room and found Sonal weeping uncontrollably, arching her body to hide her tears. Usha stood frozen. She realised then what the difference was between religious rituals and the fierce desire to love.

"Do you realise the torment they had had to endure?"

It was the evening before she was out on the field trip and Ruku was sitting in Navroj's room. He fixed his sad, listless eyes on her. Ruku's hands had slowly slipped out of his relaxed grip. She tied her long loose hair into a knot. She had shampooed her hair in the evening in anticipation of her trip; her hair was wet because of moisture in the atmosphere. As she sat with her back against the wall Ruku didn't again offer him her hand. Navroj pushed his back into his pockets and moved a few paces away. He frowned to see pieces of paper and envelopes on the floor. Like the rest, he too was preparing for his journey out, going through his papers, throwing away all that he didn't need.

"How did you come to know about all this? Must have been Kuldeep ..."

"Yes, it was – he told me everything about you and Sonal ..."

"Then, he hasn't acted as a friend ..." Navroj walked to the window turning his back at her. Evening had descended on the desolate riding ground. The long sequence of trees above the hills blended into the purplish blue of the sky, but the stars couldn't be seen through the crazed window glass.

"Kuldeep doesn't want me to love you ... do you think he has no selfish motive? I know everything ... about his love for you. He wants me out of his way."

"What are you saying, Navroj!"

Navroj made an about turn. He came at Ruku like a wounded tiger. The crazed window panes and the walls of the room disappeared behind the riot of blue and green colours of Kangra valley paintings. Holding Ruku tightly in his arms and resting his face on her shoulders, Navroj murmured, "Yes, I'm low born, I'm jealous of Kuldeep because I want you ...

I'm cured of all my illusions after seeing you. I can't think of any one else. I never thought it would be like this! I know you love me but you won't admit that ... I can see through the lie ..." Ruku didn't disengage herself from his arms or push him away. She felt she was close to the intensity of feeling itself, with his thick dark brown haired head near her face. She spoke out softly as if she were addressing his thick mop of hair, "You've given your word – your word – remember that Navroj! Sonal will die if you ..."

"I'll find a nice boy for her who belongs to her caste, a brahmin boy her mother would approve of. No matter what her mother says she regards me as a low caste boy; even my shadow pollutes their courtyard."

Suddenly Ruku broke into a loud laughter, the kind of laugh that made the next-door boy come running on winter afternoons, without his shirt on. She laughed so that her loose hair fell all over her convulsing body. She covered her face with both her hands. Navroj was stunned. He retreated red-faced. "What's the matter?"

"You're possesed by a demon, Navroj ... an evil spirit has entered your soul ..."

She tousled his hair. "Recover your wits ... we'll talk again in the morning. May I go now? Have a good trip Navroj, a happy journey," and Ruku trotted down the wooden stairs.

Mad, utterly mad this boy. Why did she have to go to his room charmed by his words? But hadn't she visited other boys before, gone into their rooms, had tea with Kuldeep and Atish, even taken a tea pot full of hot *rasam* for Murgeshan when he was down with a fever? They named her Florence Nightingale! How would she know that Navroj would break down like this and create a scene? But maybe she ought to have been more sensible. She should have guessed the storm brewing when Navroj kept on avoiding her and refused to talk to her.

Ruku posted a letter to Sonal that night, before she caught the bus to Delhi. She had got her address from Kuldeep. Sonal's reply arrived three weeks later and was lying in her post box. Then Ruku wrote back and Sonal again replied. A deep friendship was established in the process; otherwise, would Sonal have written to her about her anxieties regarding the day and time of the bethrothal? Can one talk such things except with one's dear ones? Now a photograph had accompanied a letter. Ruku felt Sonal was standing in front of her, unfolding a portrait of innocent love. That's why with some satisfaction Ruku could declare to Navroj, "That letter is *my* property now, why should I show it to you?" It seemed to her that Sonal and she were players in a team and Navroj represented the opposite side. It was at that moment Ruku came face to face with Navroj in front of Ramesh's shop. The flame of a candle threw wavering shadows in the midst of their silence. Navroj looked serious. She guessed he was feeling rather uncomfortable.

He was forking Ramesh's omlette pretending to eat; he wasn't really hungry.

"A penny for your thoughts," Ruku said.

Navroj shook his head. He wasn't thinking about anything.

"May I say something then?"

Navroj nodded looking as if he was about to receive the death sentence.

"Let's get the bethrothal ceremony over and done with before we go for our field trips, at the end of the month."

"Don't know if I can, I don't possess a penny – how can I get engaged?"

"That's no problem ... you have us with you. The academy has a guest room, the *Shivmandir* has a high priest. We'll manage. And the kind of person that you are and going so far away ... who knows you won't come across someone there, forget everything! You'll say I'm cured of all my illusions etc.,"

Navroj took hold of her wrist as she burst out laughing.

"You haven't forgiven me ..."

"What's there to forgive?" Ruku indicated for two coffees. The tip of Ramesh's nose appeared from behind the curtain. "The evil spirit in you left when you beat up Suresh Prasad to save Gauri's honour," Ruku added.

"What nonsense!" Navroj's face beamed with pride, although he felt shy and awkward.

"I have told Sonal everything about what had happened when I visited her not long ago. She was really happy about it – but went on saying no good can come out of it as the good people had had to leave and those who were bad were not thrown out. She's so innocent ... doesn't understand a thing about the intricacies of life or the political economy of the system, Ruku."

Navroj had gone straight to the North from Delhi on his way back from his village visit. He had spent a couple of days at Jammu before returning to Mussoorie. He felt he had to get his problems off his chest. Both Rukmini's rejection and the continual grudge he felt for not being able to kick that 'highly connected wheat sack' out of the academy had worn him to a frazzle. He still itched to settle scores with Suresh Prasad. He had been told in the 'Law and Order' class to use minimum force, no matter the provocation. It seemed to him that in this case the injunction was hardly fair. That was his regret. But deep within him Ruku's ringing laughter on the evening before he had departed for the village still hurt him like a thorn.

A broken-hearted Navroj had gone to Phulpur. He hadn't informed Sonal or her mother about his visit. When he reached there he saw once more the dusty courtyard and the old brick house with a tiled roof enclosed by a crumbling wall; two goats were roaming outside. It didn't look as if Usha was in. Sonal was sitting on the veranda with her arms folded around her knees and her head buried in them. Her hair looked untidy and without any oil. A shawl was flung carelessly over her shoulders. Navroj was taken back. He had never seen this Sonal! She had always appeared so neat with her hair oiled and plaited with pins, the size of drop-earings, stuck into them. Her eyes were always brightened up with kohl. The house too appeared as if it had lost all its graces: heaps of unscrubbed pots and pans lay abandoned next to the well and the string cot was upside down. He recalled how previously it was used to dry pickled lemons and chillies. There was no sign of happiness about the place.

"Sonu!"

Navroj's voice! Sonal lifted her head with a start and her lifeless plait of hair fell upon her chest. Looking at her sunken cheeks, and dark ringed eyes and look of helplessness on her face, Navroj realised the trauma she had undergone in his absence.

Yet neither Usha nor Sonal had ever mentioned their troubles in the so many letters they had written to him. They had not once mentioned the insults heaped on them by Dwivedi or their neighbours. The letters had always pressed for more of Navroj's news. They wanted to know what his life in those unfamiliar surroundings was like – the food – did he get enough to eat? Did he take a quilt to bed at night or a blanket? What did they teach him in class? etc., etc. Instantly, Navroj's imagination took a leap into some future time, twenty or thirty years from now. Rukmini had accepted him, Usha was no longer alive, Sonal was a social outcast and alone. She would perhaps keep sitting like this, her head on her lap, waiting ... her stringy, silvery-white hair would be blowing in the gust of air from the icy walls!

Sonal gave Navroj a big smile as soon as she lifted her head and saw him – the innocent smile of a twelve-year old. "I'd thought you'd never come!" It wasn't an accusation, but a hint of nightmares experienced by the girl, revealed to him in trust. They were words of a young girl, just woken up on an autumn morning. Navroj's heart began to beat fast. Standing in the dusty thresh hold, he held Sonal to him, oblivious that the door of the courtyard was ajar. He wept on her frail shoulders – tears he had held back till now, gushed forth like the dry and dusty storm. They were not aware Usha had come into the room and had gone out quietly to change her clothes.

"Sonal is so naughty, really! She told me so many things but not a word about your letter. The girl can hide!" Navroj muttered to himself while he walked back with Ruku in the dark. They were heading for their rooms. A lamp post stood next to the post office. The mountains on the other side of the road glowed in its orange light. Tufts of grass weeds and wild flowers that forced themselves out of the crevices of the path looked as if they belonged to some still-life painting in the fading brightness of the night. There was a zebra marked hump in front of them: it was for slowing down the cars at the entrance. Ruku's Block lay next to the deodar trees.

She stood at the gate, waiting to take leave of Navroj. "May I go, now?"

"You get going, I'll leave after I see you go in." And Navroj said something else about which no one knew or had heard, not even Rukmini. Watching her take the dark little road to the building made of wood and stones he had said (to himself)," Rukmini, to tell the truth, my past has gone blank. It faded into oblivion as soon as you appeared. I haven't come across anyone like you before in my life. It's you I want, and I will do so all my life ... That day you made fun of me and I listened quietly to all you had to say, but this yearning for another soul – it comes only once in life. I have kept my word. I've accepted Sonal according to your wishes. I know I have no right to hold on to you or to memories of you. But I can't give up hope so long I live. I'll take utmost care that I don't embarass you with declarations of my love."

Years later, in 1985, one autumn evening, Navroj was getting into the car, coming away from the burning ghat in the suburbs of Chandigarh. He was returning to Jaisalmer where he worked. He had watched the body of Kuldeep turn to ashes, arranged for the post-mortem, among other things. Two bullets had pierced Kuldeep's body: one had hit him in the stomach, the other, the neck. Kuldeep's smiling face amidst all the terrible pain had remained transfixed in Navroj's mind for a long time. Kuldeep still conscious had asked Navroj to bring his face close, when he went see him for the last time in the hospital. He had tried to talk, opening his mouth; his lips moved, words were released slowly.

"How's she?"

"Sonal?" Navroj knew at once Kuldeep meant some one else.

"Rukmini? She's well ... you haven't got over her as yet!"

Kuldeep couldn't move his head; he was in terrible pain. Few drops of tears had trickled down to the pillow from out of the corner of one eye. That day Navroj had little idea Kuldeep was leaving them forever ... he was thinking of staying back at Chandigarh and planning to extend his leave. As he came out of the hospital and breathed in the air of the fragrant autumn evening he recalled his own unvoiced feelings – belonging to an everning long ago, when he had stood in front of Ruku's hostel.

'This yearning for another soul – it comes but only once in one's life.'

Five

It was a cold morning in Agrahyan, although one didn't feel the weather in the town or in the market place. A wall of dense woods surrounded the bounds of the office Block, then, rather unexpectedly, there was a stretch of rice field edged by an earthen ridge where a special variety of rice grew. The field that had lain fallow at the end of harvest, was now speckledy green with peas, onions and herbs of all kinds, growing alongside. All of that was Tiwari's ancestral property and a well too. Six or seven brick-built, tin-roofed houses lay scattered in a place enclosed by a wall. Tiwari's was a Hindu undivided household: all the brothers lived together happily with their cows and bullocks. Ruku could never understand why Tiwari worked as a clerk at the Block office when he owned so much property. Tiwari was however, the Brahmin, a god, the money lender and the official authority – all rolled into one – for the illiterate peasants, the farm labourers, dalits and mundas of the village. They didn't think it was important for them to know who was the BDO of the Block: Tiwari was their undisputed ruler and the ultimate authority.

A little house rubbed against a bulwark of trees; a forest bungalow only by name. No high-ranking officer from the forest department ever stepped into the place. It had two tiny rooms, one of which was dilapidated and crumbling and not fit for living. A veranda separated the two rooms; a strip of courtyard lay in the front. The kitchen was detatched from the building. Wild thickets, prickly weeds sprang up in the space intervening the two. The dirt and cobweb festooed kitchen had borne witness to many ceremonial feasts cooked there.

A bent, bare-bodied, prickly-bearded chawkidar, wearing some officer's rejected half-pants, stood in the front of the green door of the kitchen and called out in a tremulous voice "Sir". He had a pan full of oil ready for cooking. The courtyard had a non-descript wooden gate. Its wire-netted fence had given away at places and was rolling on the ground. An emaciated-looking person wearing a white *phatua* and a white *dhoti*, stood there. He was bald with a fringe of silvery hair. The chawkidar hadn't seen him when he called out "Sir".

Rukmini, her hair uncombed and with a night dress on, peeped from behind the door she had opened a little at the noise. She couldn't see the chawkidar or his pan brimming with oil. All she noticed was the person called Gorakhprasad. Immediately she cried out, "Oh! You've been waiting so long!" She turned to the Chawkidar, "Gullu, why didn't you tell me about it? Why have you poured so much oil into the pan?" Then all at once she remembered she had asked Gulluram to prepare the dough to make *puris*. Today was Sunday. The Chawkidar brought a plate with a kilo of flour for her to see.

"How much oil have you poured, Gullu?"

"There's only a tin full. I thought I'd use up all of it."

"Good heavens, Such a lot of oil! What'll we do now?"

Gorakhprasad came forward and placed a hand on Gullu's shoulders, "Never mind, pour the oil back carefully into the tin. Take only a little ... you're cooking for one person. You don't have to cook so much food, understand?" Gorakhprasad spoke in Magdhi Hindi, what goes by the name of Maghi in that area. Gulluram was immediately put at ease; he didn't panic. A common language generally brought people close together, though that may not always be the case.

Gorakhprasad settled himself on a stool as the faint sunlight fell on the courtyard.

"I feel so guilty when I think about all the hardships you have had to put up with living in this place. At home, Babbua's mother scolds me and says we are both so selfish, we can't take care of some one who has come to us from so far. She's been frying *malpoas* since early morning. She wants you to visit us this evening ... I've come to remind you about that." Gorakhprasad was the old BDO of Duddhawa Block. He was due to retire next March. By appointing Rukmini as a trainee BDO at a time like this, the brainless people of the Capital had created havoc in the small district town as well as in Gorakhprasad's rusty household. Gorakhprasad was being transfered to the distant Champaran, which in terms of ChotaNagpur was like the North pole. He had been given three month's notice to wind up his affairs and leave. The reason why he had been ordered to go so far away was that he didn't enjoy the right political patronage. Who knew where he would finally be sent or where he might land up like a detatched kite? Gorakhprasad had been extremely agonized and filled with anger when he heard the news. He had wanted to put in his papers. Ruku had reasoned with him not to take such an extreme step; it were better to take three month's leave and stay on, she had said. Some time was required to get through with the formalities for a person to qualify for a pension. He would be harassed to no end, would have to take the bus to Delhi umpteen times and face insults and humiliating remarks at the hands of the government officials.

The old BDO quarters was fairly large. It had a number of rooms crammed with furniture. Tiwari had advised Ruku to stay there. "Why give up your style, lower your dignity, even though you've been appointed only for two months?"

Tiwari had a big nose; next to it his cunning eyes beneath his bushy eyebrows looked beady. He had pock-marked cheeks, a bald head and a pair of front teeth that seemed to bite into his drooping bottom lip. His eyes would lit up with greed when he volunteered such advice. Patting his belly with his right hand he would look as if they were about to embark upon some big enterprize. Ruku come to Gorakhprasad's quarters ignoring Tiwari's advice. Lachhmi, Gorakhprasad's wife was chopping vegetables with her head half covered. She was startled to see her and felt afraid that another calamity was about to strike them. The family had yet to recover from the devastating blow the news of Ruku's appointment and Gorakhprasad's transfer had given them. Where would they go, she with her three children, if they had to leave the house now? Ruku didn't know at that time how crushed his family were by the death of Babbua, their son: the finest offspring of Lachhmi's womb. Babbua or Arunprasad, Gorakhprasad's twentytwo year old boy, was an MA from Benaras Hindu University and an apple of his father's eye. He hadn't looked seriously for a job and was rather inclined not to work. The boy had been married off to a sixteen year-old girl when still young. The family had been looking forward to bringing the daughter-in-law home, speculating about everything they would like to do as celebration, when the tragedy struck. Gorakhprasad's three other children were much younger. There was a big age gap between Arunprasad and them. The youngest was barely ten years old.

Arunprasad had died suddenly. A temperature from the slight wound on his foot had developed into tetanus, and he had a painful death in the hospital. Gorakhprasad was out of the house then and Lachhmi was given news of his death by strangers returning from the hospital. It seemed to her that a fierce dust storm had ripped off the fruit of her love. After that Lachhmi herself had became very frail, and like some bereaved animal had been almost on the point of death. When Ruku came upon her she could hardly stand on her feet. Continually afraid that further calamity was in store, she lived in a state of apprehension.

Ruku least wanted to turn Gorakhprasad and his family out of what had been their home. What would she – a single woman – do with a big house? Besides there was this forest lodge. Why must she thrust herself on them?

"Then you must eat every meal with us ..." Lachhmi demanded in her usual unreasonable manner. How could that be? It was impossible for Ruku to make Lachhmi, as old as her own mother, understand that with all the treking she had to do in the woods and the mountains and the inclement climate she had had to cope with she simply had no time to think about food. She was not a bit concerned about getting proper meals at the right time. Now they had managed to arrive at a mutually pleasing arrangement: Lachhmi packed and sent her all the delicacies she prepared, Gulluram warmed up the food and served. Gullu had also learnt how to cook a bit, but more than often it was Ruku who went into the kitchen after her day's work was done and cooked for herself.

Gulluram's apprehensions were of a different kind – he was a Harijan. Even the water he touched was considered polluted. At first he hinted about this to Ruku. When that failed, he revealed his fears completely. That brought him no respite!

Ruku said, "I'll drink water from the hand of whoever I choose ..."

Gullu still hesitated, "But I know nothing about cooking ..."

"I'll teach you how to cook ... will you?"

Tiwari produced a Brahmin, from lord knows where, with a dhoti down too his knees and a filthy thread around his neck. "He'll do your cooking Madam, he's a good cook, comes from the neighbouring village of Saru. He's a Matric-failed unemployed youth," he said.

"Don't bother about it – there's Gullu," Ruku replied

Tiwari's face turned owlish, his broomstick brows stood on their edge as he whispered, "But what'll people say? Have you given that a thought? You're a Brahmin, on top of it a woman ... you must follow the norms and customs of your caste, maintain the dignity of society. You are the ruler in this place after all."

Ruku stopped abruptly eating roti and gur; she laughed scornfully moving her body like the yellow of the mustard fields.

"Wonderful Tiwariji – woman, Brahmin, ruler – what a fantastic blend of properties! As for the contradictions – does one have to protect one's caste to remain respectable?"

A bashful Tiwari with his brahmin cook made an immediate exit while Gulluram joyfully spiced up the *khichuri* with his dirty hands. Days passed.

Today, chewing the fennel seed stuffing of the *malpoa* in Gorakhprasad's house, Ruku noticed that they were preparing to depart. The packing had begun. Items in the bedroom were already assembled together and a jute sack covering lay on the floor. Gorakhprasad himself replied to her unvoiced question.

"It's *Poush* next month. We can't travel then. Babbua's mother observes all the customs even if I don't. To her the months of *Poush*, *Chaitra* and *Bhadra* are unlucky. We plan to leave in *Magh*."

"How can that be? You haven't given up the idea of leaving after my telling you so many times not to?"

"No Madam, I don't like it here anymore. I drag myself to the office every morning. There is such a lot of tension between me and the members of the panchayat committee and the MLAs – how long can I cope? Babbua's death has left a void in my heart. I am like an insect-ravaged grain of rice; what you see is only husk. I was attached to the place because the village folk had put up a headstone on the bank of the river Badki for Babbua. I felt he lay there, my dear boy! I couldn't go away leaving him behind. I have regained my courage after I met you. I now know that the world is a big place – there are good men to counter the bad ones. I also know that I can establish a deep bond with a total stranger. It's a small world – we are in it together."

Ruku had on different occasions heard all kinds of stories about Gorakhprasad from all kinds of people. He had been a bigboned man and not thin and frail or bow-backed as he was now; some one with big bones and a sharp nose was uncommon among the illiterate undeveloped people. But Gorakhprasad came from the Northern lowlands where water from the river made year-round cultivation of land possible. The rich people there, like Ruku and her people from Calcutta, couldn't do without boiled rice or fish curry. People in the South are always uncomfortable about the Northerners and find the harsh decisions they make rather unpalatable. As for the politicians – they calculate what is near to them and what is far, not in terms of districts or states but according to the borderline of the panchayat villages. People from the neighbouring states are treated as strangers. There is hardly any difference, in this respect, between the ministers and members of legislative assemblies. Ministers also nurse their constituencies for votes.

In spite of the inexorable march of social change, Gorakhprasad had been acceptable to the local people. He didn't talk big, worked hard all day long and was extremely daring; he scouted the entire locality all by himself, undaunted by wild rivers or rugged mountains. What people didn't appreciate was his honesty and scruple in handling government money. "All government officers made money on the side, would work get done otherwise? No person would come forward with a proposal for development if money were not exchanged under the counter," they had declared. On his part Gorakhprasad hadn't even managed to acquire an acre of land anywhere. All he had was his dilapidated ancestral house. The rich Rajputs, Kayestha government officers, the Koeris or the Kurmis could hardly describe him as 'a lion of a man;' secretely they said he was a worm. How could a person who had not seen better days know how to make money? He had got his son married without accepting a penny and now goes about in his old age like a beggar with no future.

Gorakhprasad couldn't care less about all that people said about him. The clan had rejected him a long time ago, when they realised that he was getting transferred from place to place and had been finally banished to the Adivasi inhabited southern part of Chota Nagpur and that he didn't have political patrons. Lachhmi, however, never complained about his obstinacy or his lack of support where she was concerned. His honesty was the sole source of her joy and pride. She could never buy any jewellery when she wanted to and didn't make a fuss if she had to sell some when they fell short of money. Daughters of well-to-do parents would have buried their heads in shame had they faced a similar situation. Gorakhprasad didn't feel conscience-striken for not doing anything to lessen the burden of Lachhmi's domestic chores, or for not being able to adorn her with beautiful sarees and jewellery. Like the war-horse that he was, he remained constantly alert for the call of the trumpet. Babbua's death had destroyed his pride; he had felt bewildered and defeated. He was now like a reined-in blindfolded horse.

The shefali flowers were still blossoming and waves of fragrance from shefali trees haunted the village track. Ruku came across an impenetrable mass of old trees closing in all sides of Gorakhprasad's house – *ber*, *arjun* and banana trees loomed in front of her. She couldn't see a thing! Ruku didn't carry a torch and Gorakhprasad insisted his third son escort her with a lantern. "Why bother? I'm used to going about alone in this wild place – the woods and jungles – as if you don't know." Gorakhprasad stood quietly for a few minutes on the threshold then softly replied, "I know that ... but how can I, as a father, not care?" He was suddenly embarassed.

It was getting cold; the early morning dew fell on the grass, on the scattered blossoms and the leaves of the ponticia plant. The migratory birds had long since left the snowy regions for the warmer countries. In a few days time the mountain springs of the plateau would resonate with sounds of their flapping wings. Ruku covered her head with a shawl; the cardigan she had on was not enough to protect her from the biting cold. The young boy who followed her had a monkey cap on at his mother's insistence. The faint yellow beam from his soot-covered lantern swayed, keeping rhythm with his enigmatic shadow. The snakes lay dormant in the earth during winter months, as for the loamy field rats – their reign was over with the end of the harvest season.

What a swift change of scenes! The lanscape alters and along with it the procession of strange human faces! Ruku lay on her hard bed contemplating the different experiences she had had under gone. Do human beings also change, forget the past as they get involved in the joys and sorrows of different people in strange lands and unfamiliar places? Just a few months ago at this hour she was at the Ladies' Block, gazing at the milky-white shadows of the table lamp on the wall. She had gone to sleep resting her head on the lacy pillow cover, listening to songs or reading *The Economic and Political Weekly*.

The carpet on the floor was meant to insulate the room

from the cold; on top of it she could use the room heater. She had heard sounds of heavy mountain showers, the cry of the night birds on the deodar trees and the squeaky noise of wooden boards of the balcony; the sharp clatter of stilleto heels blended with the squashy tread of canvas shoes. Small and slim Ila Gibbs had wrapped herself up in a huge quilt and had whistled into her ears. Ila, a girl belonging to a Telengana Christian family, had had to put up with so many insults at the house of the North Indian Brahmin, Amaresh Tripathi – all because she was in love with him. She used to get ugly letters with dire warnings and threats all the time. But that bustling creature had still managed to make people laugh! Why was it that Ruku thought about her at a time like this?

The window on top of her bed didn't open; the other window in her bedroom had to be kept shut because of the cold. The bed creaked as Ruku turned on her side – it was an ordinary bed. She could do with freshly laundered sheets and pillow cases but Ruku never remembered to do the washing. Gullu had become so afraid of her that he daren't enter her room. The mosquito net was new; her mother had given it to her when she in Calcutta not long ago.

Ruku had arrived at Duddhawa Block early October. It was a place on the periphery of a deep forest, in the district of Hazaribagh. She had to give up the idea of going to Calcutta for the Pujas. There was no time for that. It was her first experience of being away from home during the festival Season; she was not even aware that the mildly fragrant month of *Ashwin* had come and gone. Hazaribagh! To reach the place she had to first take the train to Ranchi then travel three and a half hours by bus. She could have spent a day in Calcutta if she had three free days. Babai had said, "You won't be able to put up with all the strain ... you've already travelled so much, why not stay, we'll miss you when you're gone!"

Ruku had spent ten days in Calcutta at the end of July when there were heavy rains. The broken concrete footpaths of Calcutta streets spattered with muck and slime. The silhuette of the grimy city stuck out against the sky. Clothes never seemed to dry but wasn't she happy! She was back in home town after such a long time. This was the world to which she belonged. She didn't have to say 'sorry' if she stumbled or dip her hands into the finger bowl at the end of a meal. She could happily lick roasted aubergine off her fingers or sing as and when she pleased. Ma and Umamashi heard her talk about the mountains with their eyes wide open. They asked her questions that made Ruku's sides split or which made her see red. They always sat down for dinner together, either at Umamashi's or at home.

Ruku had noticed Phalgun hurrying over his meals and retiring into a corner with a book, pretending to read. He had been turning pages of the book rapidly. But Ruku had felt his eyes were transfixed on her, as if all his senses were focused into his gaze. She had felt a sudden thrill and stopped talking. Umamashi and Ma had asked her what was the matter.

Ruku couldn't describe what she felt to any one, least of all to her mother. She had travelled to distant lands, come across many renowned men. She had seen from extremely close quarters – the way they behaved, went about, their style and their self esteem. She had come close to love but they didn't look at her in the way Phalgun did. Their silence, their sitting alone otherwise engaged, had not touched her heart in the way Phalgun did.

When on the wet *Shraban* day the train splashed by rain was about to pull in at Howrah station, resting her chin on the window, Ruku had seen Baba and Umamashi on the platform and at some distance, two absent-minded, calm lotus-like eyes. Baba looked about espectantly; he hadn't seen her for such a long time. But forgetting everything Ruku had jumped out of her compartment like the paratroopers on the green rice fields, and had shouted Phalgu-u-n! Immediately a lock of hair fell on to the boy's forehead. He had seen her – he ran alongside the still moving train as if half of his soul had been running parallel to Ruku's. By then Ruku's heart was aglow with a dazzling light and she could weave into herself the narrative of her return in the sun and the wind. That day she had realized that her joy and the thrill she had felt were inextricably linked with her self discovery, the knowledge of who she was.

That feeling intensified in the days she spent in Calcutta, although she was caught up in a whirlwind of activities – excessive parental attention, dinners at the homes of relatives, packing for the journey to Hazaribagh. She had had Phalgun to herself only for two days. She had talked to him lying on his bed when Ma and Umamashi had gone to Gariahata. Facing him she had related the entire history of Navroj, the drama surrounding Sankaran's resignation and Suresh Prasad's heroics. Phalgun had listened to all she said with close attention, holding her hand. Then at one moment her head had fallen on his arm; soon she was breathing deeply in sleep. Ma came and woke her up. "Get up, come and eat! Must I carry around such a big girl!" A wet monsoon breeze flowed into the room, Phalgun had got up and left, covering her with his own light toosh shawl.

The second time they were together was the day before she came away to Hazaribagh. Phalgun was playing in a concert in the Gorki Sadan Hall. Ruku had attended the concert alone as Ma and Baba were not interested in coming, Umamashi who went to the gate of Gorki Sadan with her also left, fondling her hair and saying, "I've work to do." The group of musicians had among them those from Calcutta School of Music, some old teachers and one or two composers who didn't belong to the band. Phalgun, Deep Parekh and one other unknown boy played Vivaldi's *Spring Quartet*, Mozart's *Eine Kleine* and Bach's *Sleepers Wake*, on the violin.

When Ruku had listened to Phalgun playing music, sitting alone in half-shadow, by the window of his room, she had thought of him as a piece of white cloud floating suspended in the sky. There was nothing to single him out. But today, she saw the same lonesome youth, wrapt in music played by eighteen men with their flutes, the cello, violins and the piano; she felt he had created the melody just for her and she knew instantly the reason why Umamashi hadn't wanted to come to the concert. She was his mother after all. Vivaldi's *Spring*

Quartet had carried Phalgun to the region of variegated light and shadow, to the deep blue sky, like some dust-coated leaf whirled around by the storm. Ruku had never beheld any person express such an exuberant joy of music, especially someone as serene as Phalgun.

Ruku had returned home to find her mother looking glum, her father lying on the bed and reading.

"You'll be going away after a day, when are going to have some time for us or do the packing?"

"Bah! didn't you say you'd be cooking *biriyani* and rather stay at home?"

She understood that her mother had noticed she and Phalgun had walked home together and talked intimately, standing for a long time below the staircase in the dark.

A vague anxiety had got hold of her mother. She worried that their relationship was developing in a way that may affect both their lives. What would happen to Ruku's 'grand' future then? Her social standing? What would the relatives say? Her mother's feelings were as yet unclear but Ruku had no doubt this was the way her thoughts ran. She felt a mingled pain, both for her mother now that she was about to cut the umbilical cord and land in Phalgun's world and for Umamashi who was terrified Ruku would take Phalgun away from her. Ruku's childhood and adoleseence – all those days of play and laughter – had been fortified by the love of those two women. Now a crack had appeared in their love for her, like the breach in the Berlin Wall before it was pulled down.

Ruku wasn't agonized about Phalgun; she couldn't think of

herself as someone separate from him. Her difficulties and his sufferings seemed to have finally coalesced. It didn't matter to her now that she had him to herself for such brief moments; there was no essential difference between their coming together momentarily and their living till eternity with each other. The train to Ranchi had pulled out of the platform and lost itself in the full-moon lit fields carrying Ruku immersed in such dreams.

The autumn air was alive with the feel of *Puja,* Ruku felt a surge of longing within her. She couldn't hear recitations of the *Chandi* texts here, no *Mahalaya* songs reverberated in the air in the mornings, but when she heard the birds warble. she knew the days of Goddess Durga had arrived. Mother would be up early to go to Kalighat and make her offerings. Ruku had heard the rustle of her *garad* silk saree when she lay in bed, a child still. She had heard the shefali flowers unfold, seen blossoms scattered on the ground like stars and had stepped over them carefully so as not to crush them, Memories of childhood and adolescence appeared in a row in her mind's eye. These were entertwined with her growing up with Phalgun beside her. In spite of a deep conviction that they were together forever – it made little diffenence whether they saw each other or not – Ruku yearned to see him. She longed for another glimpse of that face, those eyes sorrowful like the fields robbed of sunlight at dusk. She felt restless.

As she thumbed the dusty files, listened to the talk of the Chief Officer or the enlightened conversation of the clerks sitting at the back and dissected the cases of illegal land occupation, Ruku realised all her thoughts were focused elsewhere, on a face that overshadowed the old illegible village maps. When the train for Ranchi had left the Howrah Station and the sky, aglow with light, had gone out of focus to her tear-filled eyes, a voice had cried out within her asking, "Why? Why was she always lacerated like this?" Why couldn't she stay at home beside the person she longed for? That wrenching feeling had got somewhat abated as she became busy with work. Today, the smell of autumn redolent with the scent of the *pujas* once again summoned it up.

Ruku had no leave days left to take a holiday. The period of field training was bound by a tight schedule. Nevertheless she would have run home if only Baba had asked her – he didn't. On the contrary he suggested she didn't come as the journey to Calcutta would be too tiring for her. Much later Ruku realized her mother had spoken to her father and must have expressed her anxieties in that particular way. It was hardly likely Baba would have had such thoughts. He had only expressed Ma's feelings.

Her parents are always happy when she goes home. They look several years younger. Baba goes to the market a hundred times a day. Ma exudes that indescribable smell Ruku associated with lying on her lap on winter afternoons. It was going to be lonely Puja for them this time around, with the small comfort that their daughter wouldn't be seeing Phalgun. She felt slighly unhappy about the changed circumstances.

Thakurdas Ganguli carried on his familial Durga worship in the hall of his ancestral home. He invited Ruku to join him for an afternoon meal on the day of *Ashtami*. The Ganguli matron was fair complexioned. The garad silk saree she wore made her look even more resplendent. The golden bangles around her plump hands and a double chin suggested boundless peace and prosperity. The goddess had elongated yellow eyes and stood over a green demon. People swarmed all over the place. Ruku could hear the clamour of the drummers, the clashing of cymbals and the music of the shenai. Grief and lonliness came in waves as she rolled *mohanbhog* inside the *puris*.

Who were these people? Why was she here? Where should she have been? *Puris* tumbled out of wicker baskets onto her plate, her silence seemed to encourage those who served the meal. The *puris* were left untouched making Ganguli matron feel extremely discomfitted.

Ruku was packed and ready to take over as the development and revenue circle officer of the Duddhawa Block by the time the full moon had begun to wane – during the month of *Aswin*. She had to learn to work at the grass-root level, a difficult job as she would have to be completely on her own. Ruku was ready to take the plunge but the official order had yet to arrive. Both the Divisional Commissioner Surajprasad Jha and M.P. Rathindra had their reservations about sending her so far. Who would protect her in the wild mountainous place, at least forty miles into the interior? They didn't even know where she would stay. Finally district administrator Amit Sen put down his foot, he said angrily, "Why make so much fuss about her security – no one has to bother his head about her, Rukmini can look after herself. It's not that she is being sent to another planet! Isn't Duddhawa in our district? Go Ruku – go and pack up."

Amit Sen was small and fat and had a big moustache. He wore thick glasses through which he looked at everyone sternly. Ruku had been disciplined by his strict regime although he was only six years older than her. The office of the DM was attached to the District office; there were besides a dozen executive magistrates, a civil supply officer and a chief medical officer. The DM was the smallest in size among them yet he weilded an authority that made others shake in their boots. Amit had taken Ruku under his wings to shape her up for the worst possible scenario. He seemed to constantly hold her at gun point. She was in his line of fire if she arrived five minutes late for meetings or inspection tours. However, at times he also fed her with home-made parathas and vegetable cutlets. He would proclaim, "Don't think you can get by just because you're a woman, you musn't be guilty of dereliction of duty. Be alert." And with those words hand her a plate of stale locally made biscuits.

While at Mussoorie, Ruku had heard that training officers (referred to as assistant magistrates), were treated as the sons-in-law of the entire district. They were invited to all the parties. People's hearts melted if they bunked office work and went to matinee shows. A brand new jeep was kept ready for their use. The trainee officers were mollycoddled most at a time when the situation demanded an imposition of law and order. But Ruku was a woman – how could she expect such luck? Her fate was to be treated as the daughter-in-law and suffer constant harassment. Hardly she was back from the land acquisition camp than Amit Sen was ready to take her to the place where the real battle was on. She had to sit with the district judge and learn how to dispense judgements. She had to go about the entire district, visit the headquarter and all the offices. The rattling jeep was not always there for her trips but Amit Sen had given clear orders she had to take the bus if the jeep was not available.

Never mind – a hardened and resilient Ruku had gone off to Duddhawa without a care, feeling a wee bit sad somewhere in her heart. She had got attached to the room in the corner of the Circuit House during her three months stay in the place. She had cooked lightheartedly in a little stove in the make-shift kitchen in the iron grilled balcony, covered with sheets and canvas. A curly-headed slim boy called Ikram (the name was actually Akram), had been at her beck and call. On days the head clerk Mower Sahib strode in. Ikram's job depended on his will and whim. Mower Sahib could get him any job he wanted with a simple flourish of his pen. Ikram was a day-labourer – he had to part with a portion of his earning to the Babus as commission. He could never keep his accounts straight.

That little kitchen, the tarnished mirror on the dressing table – she had become so attached to them. She had felt so sad when she glanced at the room while she sat and packed on the open veranda. The room seemed a part of herself she was going to leave behind.

They had meant to set out early; the journey to Duddhawa

got delayed for several reasons. By the time they got started a cold air had started to blow. They took a gravelled path that made its way to the main road half-circling the Circuit House and going around the garden. Thick woods on the left rubbed against a forest of *sal* and *arjun* trees. As the car took a left turn Ruku suddenly remembered one night of heavy rains when she had just arrived at the place. She had seen an old mango tree next to the yellow building in all its heavenly splendour. Millions of fireflies glowed brightly all over the top of the tree, its trunk dug deep into the wet earth, in the moisture laden atmosphere. Ruku had never seen so many fireflies at one time.

The road gradually melted into the plateau of Chota Nagpur, then rolled out of the town. The sprawling unsown fields on either side were fringed by *babla* bushes, the horizon of a mountain range lay at a distance. At times the road came perilously close to dark woods where the bright moon shone solemnly overhead. The smell of cooked lentils spiced up with *panchforon* hit her nostrils as they came upon a level crossing and had to wait for the gates to reopen. The tarred road finally came to an end and gave itself up to an uneven mud track – by then the night had deepened. Ruku's throat had begun to feel sore and her cheeks had got frozen due to the cold breeze from the hills. When the bright beams of the full moon cascaded – the trees, the thickets and all the houses were covered with a film of light. It was then she saw a kerosene lamp burning dimly in a scattered market place, noticed the few rows of shops as the car entered the jurisdiction of the Duddhawa

Block. There – was the ghost of a forest bungalow! She had to build a home here, make her bed, bring to the place all the things she might need to make life passable. She felt utterly alone in this world of darkness as the jeep roared to go back.

By the middle of December Ruku began to feel she had become physically weak; hard work didn't enfeeble any one. Lack of love and loss of inspiration had made Ruku worn out. She hadn't seen Phalgun for such a long time, nor was there any possibility of meeting him in the near future so that her batteries might get recharged. All she had as resource were the few blue letters, damp with dew. But words had no meaning when not matched by things seen.

The non-gazetted officers had gone on a strike at the beginning of the month. The office was deserted – Bhola, Nareshbabu, Syed, Tiwariji were absent. The driver Kishanlall had also left one morning, leaving the car key with her. Kishanlall didn't want to go off work – what choice did he have when it was a question of solidarity with the officers of the federation who had called the strike? Ruku worked alone. She opened the files, read the letters, kept hand written records and drafts, made notes; she had to even open the office premises in the morning. The bulbs in the building had fused. Ruku kept candles burning throughout the day. The only saving feature of the situation was the police van Amit Sen had left behind for her use.

Gulluram cooked so badly that food was inedible. Ruku had to return home, light the firewood and cook for herself. It was then that she felt lonely, drained of physical energy. A meeting had taken place some days ago where the Chief Minister expressed his wish to increase the yield of potato crops in the district. More land had to be brought under potato cultivation. The Minister targeted those farmers who could till more hectors of land. Ruku's head swam – no one at the meeting had spoken a word against the proposal; any minor objection were brushed under the carpet. As Amit Sen left the place, the District Agriculture Officer started to make big noises. He claimed that there would be a record of sorts in potato cultivation that year. The government of Haryana had promised to despatch seeds that gave higher yield; the seeds would arrive any day now. The farmers were asked to gear themselves up for the big job. He calculated and wrote down in detail how to distribute the seeds. Some farmers would get twenty tons, others twelve or fifteen – no one would receive less than ten tons, otherwise it would be impossible to save face. The farmers had to make use of the entire stock of seeds donated to them.

How much land was required for potato farming? A plan was drawn up about the amount of seeds per acre.

But the Agriculture Officer Mahato was not pleased with the estimated area under potato for Duddhawa. The size of the ground to be cultivated seemed to him too small; they had cultivated double the area last year. He told Ruku, "You're new here, how'll you know? We must lift at least fifteen tons of the seeds." That meeting with the Minister had taken place days before Ruku took over the affairs of the district, but the seeds had yet to arrive.

"The planting season is almost over – when are you going to sow the seeds?" Ruku couldn't help asking. Some officers started chewing their pencils, others drummed their fingers on the table. Mahato pulled a long face and said, "Use your influence, call the peasants, arrange a meeting – the planting season is not important, what is – is that the Government has given us its word."

Ruku had quickly summoned the peasants, many of whom were Tiwari's friends or buddies. They came with their turbans tightly perched on their heads and uttered words of wisdom, stroking their unshaven cheeks. To them it was a matter of prestige. They were willing to reduce the area of other vegetable farming in order to leave land for growing potatoes. But the seeds must be made available without delay.

It was already the middle of October and according to the rural calendar the days for potato cultivation was coming to an end – that was a month ago. By now even that was forgotten; farmers were planting whatever they pleased. They were in the middle of the *ravi* season. All kinds of thoughts swarmed in Ruku's head. The potato seeds hadn't arrived. So much the better. With the officers on strike who was there to take them?

Four days ago Tiwari appeared balancing a cake of *gur* on his hands. He said, "Typical ... the government always makes empty promises! Two and half bighas of my land is lying fallow for potatoes – who'll compensate me for the loss?"

"What is the price of the *gur*, Tiwariji?"

"Don't even mention – such a small thing."

"I've told you I can't accept gifts, others might notice and bring me things. Tell me how much do I owe you." "Throw a small amount of money if you must – it's peanuts for you. Fifty rupees. I'll give it to Lachhman, my labourer who brought it."

Tiwari always brought her small gifts – half a cake of jaggery or fresh mustard oil from the mill. He always made the excuse they came from home. He stayed glum faced for three days running if she refused to accept them. Ruku made a pact with him. Tiwari had to accept money in exchange for gifts. She thought this would settle him, once and for all. But the effect was quite different. Tiwari started quoting three times the market price. Ruku was beguiled. His attitude would be understandable if he was poor and wanted to keep some money for himself. But Tiwari was filthy rich!

Gorakhprasad came and warned her.

"It's not nice to speak ill of a person but people say Tiwari makes a lot of money on the side. He's intoxicated by wealth, lends money to others on high interest. Be careful, be careful, Madam, tighten you belt." Ruku was amazed. Here she was, at an old dilapidated building in the midst of nowhere, Gulluram, her constant companion's speech was so slurred that it was hardly intelligible yet rumours about her got around. There was no news that didn't reach their ears. She recalled what Sankaran had once said in the lecture Hall of the Academy: "You'll be the center of attention in small districts, sub-divisional towns and Block offices. How you live, whom you see, your dress, the food you eat – all this would be grist to the country folk's mill. In the eyes of the people you are the government. They will judge the system – its health, how it is working, from the way you conduct yourself. Only when you are back in Delhi will you be free from this kind of constant surveillance, untill then – be careful."

Ruku took rupees fifteen out of her bag. "The market price for the jaggery is twelve, I am giving you a few extra rupees. Tell Lachhman he musn't buy at such high price," she said. Tiwari pushed the money into his pocket looking rather sheepish. After that, there was no further discussion about potato farming. Ruku concluded she had won the first round of the battle by putting a price tag on Tiwari's gift.

A shivering *Paush* night! Numb with the cold Ruku was trying desparately to go to sleep. Although all the windows of the room were shut, cold invaded her body like a wild boar if there was so much as a hair-line gap among the layers of cotton of the quilt. The portion of bed below her got ice cold when she changed sides. She felt sure the mountain streams were frozen and had become as hard as ice pick. Wind from those regions were cutting across the tableland like a whip. In the evening she had seen an elephant sitting on the ground next to the building, looking like a grey ghost; the mahut was lighting a little fire at a distance. They must have got back from some village fair. Elephants carried money, rice, coconuts and whatever else the village folk give, with their trunks. Who knew where the mahut would put up for the night? It was so bitterly cold!

Phalgun owned a big quilt made out of flowery satin material. Rukmini snuggled down under it in her thoughts and went off to sleep.

Calcutta never got cold. She never had to cope with such loneliness there. The bed hadn't seemed so empty. It was past midnight. Silence reigned everywhere; not a single twitter of the birds could be heard. Rukmini heard muffled indistinct noises in her dreams.

"Get up, get up, Madam – the potatoes are here." Ruku got up with a bustle and put on one of her heavy sweaters. She lit the veranda lamp and took out the torch she kept under her pillow as soon as she unlatched her bedroom door. The chill outside made her shrink. There was no light in the courtyard. She beamed the torch on Gulluram's startled face and behind him on the monkey capped, shawl wrapped, massively built Haryana driver's tired red eyes. The driver held a piece of crumpled paper in his hand.

"Take this – it's the consignment note. Make arrangements for the delivery, madam, and let me go. I have had to travel a long way to get here."

Twelve tons of potato seeds – at the end of December!

The truck had finally arrived. It had left Haryana, crossed Uttar Pradesh, halted at Ranch, colliding again and again with the darkness covering much of the forest area. Ruku suddenly remembered Mahato's words. "The season is not important – we have to see whether the government means business.'

A shivering half-pant clad Gulluram went out in the dark to look for Nareshbabu. He had the godown keys. A striking officer, Naresh opened the godown, wearing a thick dhoti, a shawl and a cap. The lid of the truck was taken off and millions of potato seeds, tied in sacks, rolled into the godown raising a lot of dust. By then Ruku was properly clad and ready to take over the business. The truck roared and came to a stop near the office as the godown was full up. More storage space had to be found.

An old office room stacked with old files – there were brooms, phenyle, dusters and soaps besides – potatos got unloaded in their midst. Soon all that space was taken up. Potatos tumbled into Ruku's personal office. The sacks had come open and the potatoes enjoying their freedom jumped out in glee. They gathered beneath her revolving chair and formed a mound as if they were stone pebbles.

Gulluram lit the stove and produced hot tea. Early morning tea made everyone happy – the driver, the helper, Nareshbabu and the mahut. The truck was empty. The representative from Haryana could go home happy, his job was done.

Ruku looked up and saw the mist-covered darkness outside and above. How could she swallow her embarrassment and call the peasants over to the place – now? She thought about the situation. Perhaps she had to send for them; what other way was there for her? And what was in store – for her? Boiled potatoes, fried potatoes, and potatoes made into a curry? If she counted all the people in the village how many potatoes would each one of them get? One or two?

Sticking her feet under the quilt Ruku began a long letter. A letter with documentary details about *l' affaire des pommes de terre* – for Phalgun's benefit, ofcourse!

Six

In the morning mist the two houses looked exactly alike, and the mist turned into a smoky blue haze as the light from street lamps fell on it. One of the houses was a long, narrow, double storied building, the other had only one floor. The boundary walls of the terrace hadn't been given a plaster for some time. A detatched yellow kite from last years Viswakarma puja could be seen from the window of the attic room. A dust and cobweb covered top lay slanted next to it. Once upon a time a little girl had called the spider's web *buji*; she had just began to join words together. She used cover to her eyes with both her hands in fright. Phalgun designed this kite last year. Ruku held on to its top while he flew it in the wind. She was no longer the little girl who had made the *buji* sound.

A plant shoots upwards, grows tall, as its roots break out of the split seed – it is in the nature of things. But Ruku's growing up produced a hiatus in the two houses: a crack not visible in the morning mist but pronounced in daylight. The old man from the countryside who came with fresh date sugar in little earthen bowls hadn't visited for a long time. He had his daughter's marriage to fix, dowry money to scratch up. He had an ugly scuffle with his daughter's would – be, mean, father-in-law over alloy in the gold ring he had given.

The old man had acquired a *panjabi* from Ruku's father so that he could look respectable in society. He appeared after a long gap. He couldn't recollect Calcutta so cold in this winter. He had a ragged sweater on and a scarf over his head; he felt cold all the same. His grandsons were little scoundrels – happily frittering away their time smoking or playing cards. They refused to help him carry the wicker basket, full of cakes made out of date sugar. He had so many mouths to feed at home; he had to be not only out on the streets but cook as well, after wife's death. He drew deep breaths as he struggled up the stairs of the two storied house and sat down to take some rest. He had undone his scarf and put down the basket. What a pity nobody wanted a *moa* or a *chandrapuli* any more! He had brought along a cake of date sugar and thin molasses for the family and had noticed the lock hanging on the door of the next house; the one which had only one floor. He placed two one *seer* pots of molasses alongside. "Aren't you going to pay me, Ma?" he asked.

Ruku's mother Chitra picked up a pot and paid for it. The old man's mouth was wide open in surprise. It was something the like of which he had never experienced before, not during the fifteen years of his visiting the place.

" The house is locked up, Ma, must I take all this fresh *gur* back? Couldn't you keep it for them?"

He had left things for both the houses in one place so many times in the past. But Chitra was visibly displeased and went inside. The world was no longer the same the old man thought to himself. He hadn't seen the thin, pale, bespectacled girl for a long time. She would call him grandad and say, "Why don't you put less sugar in the *chandrapuli* so that I can eat?" The narrow double-storied building looked really eerie since the girl left – its doors and windows dreadfully still and shut all the time. There must have been some misunderstanding between the two houses – something to do with the girl's going away, the old man thought in a vague fashion. He loosened the red thread with which the arms of his glasses were kept attached and thought about other things. He must ask his son to get him a new pair of specs even though he wouldn't provide him with a new set of teeth. He must insist on that as soon as he got home and then a roaring fight would ensue between father and son.

Uma was returning home having collected the milk and shopped for food. She had locked up her house because Phalgun had gone out so early in the morning. Her shopping bag felt heavy with the season's vegetables. She hadn't found her way into the fishmarket, thick with people. She held a bottle of milk covered with muddy water on the other hand. Now she had to balance the one *seer* earthen pot of *gur* on its top. That stubborn old man had simply thrust the pot at her and taken the money when she came by him on the street. Chitra had refused to accept it on her behalf. Uma's ears reddened as the man recited the events, standing in front of the shops. Her back got wet with perspiration in spite of the cold. Uma was getting on in years; she tired easily when she lugged the shopping. She didn't feel happy about it. Her knees ached and she suffered from cramps at night but she had to look after everything to do with the house, all by herself. Phalgun did help with the marketing when he didn't have to rush out early.

She tried to remember the eons of year she had been walking to the market like now. When was it that she had begun to do the shopping? Perhaps the year Phalgun's father died and she was not more than thirty two years old. Her son was just three then. Ananda loved to hear his baby voice – trying hard to form full sentences. He sounded so sweet! When a year and a half, the child could reproduce with ease the opening notes of Beethoven's *Pastoral.* Ananda listened to the Friday late-night western classical music that was put on request in channel B of Calcutta radio, with Phalgun lying on his back, face buried. That was Phalgun's initiation into music. His voice lost its tonal quality as he grew older and faded away like the sun on a cloudy day. It was Mritunjoy who taught him how to play the flute. Uma hadn't agreed and Chitra and co., worried it would be hard on his lungs and he become weak.

Mritunjoy taught Indian classical music on the harmonium; he also played the flute. He lived in the neighbourhood and ran a small music school in a little two-storied building, at the crossing of Harish Mukherjee and Hazra Road. What with running of the house, bringing up the son, and keeping her school job after the death of her husband, Uma was left with no time for anything; she hadn't a breathing space. Mritunjoy put the violin into the hands of a ten-year old boy. And simultaneously Phalgun discovered the Calcutta School of Music. Every other day he would return from school, wash his face, fool around in the neighbouring house and run to the school with his violin.

Phalgun had never played cricket with the children of his locality on winter afternoons; he never reveled in *guli-danda.* Uma knew the local boys were not his friends but Phalgun was of gentle and quiet nature, he laughed and spoke nicely to everyone. Among his school chums, Rana and Kishore came home. Kishore was mischievous and eccentric, Rana clever and indifferent to studies. Kishore wore thick glasses, wasn't bothered about passing or failing an exam. He got left behind and gradually dropped out of school. But Phalgun wasn't close to either; his thoughts were centered only on one person. Uma knew that well. The boy was thoroughly absorbed in Rukmini, a girl two years his younger. She seemed to keep him enthralled. Uma hadn't been happy about her son's single-minded devotion to the girl but feeling very affectionate towards her herself, she didn't let it unduly worry her. Rather, she was happy and resigned to the idea that Rukmini was Phalgun's fate.

It was Ruku's parents and not Uma who were so upset when Phalgun failed to secure a first in his Higher Secondary exam, Uma hadn't failed to notice. Ruku's father Arun was quite harsh to Phalgun amidst all his show of affection. Phalgun heard him with his head hung low. Rukmini cried her heart out. Uma had fed Ruku with food especially cooked for her when she was admitted to Presidency college. Phalgun had arranged the table and decorated the place with colourful streamers – that was his way of celebrating he told her. Then Uma had to feed both of them, pressing the rice into tiny round balls, so that the two didn't start a fight!

Uma recalled how angry Arun was even as she placed the pot of molasses on top of her shopping bag. Why must the people next door turn their heat on Phalgun as Ruku became more and more successful? How was the boy to blame? Now that Rukmini has spread out her wings and glided into the horizon of vast possibilities. The people of both the houses, had finalised Ruku's departure plans, had felt sad in equal measure when she left, had avoided each other's eyes lest one or the other gave in to feelings of dejection. Letters arrived at regular intervals – blue envelopes, white ones, at times just inland letters. Together they had read what she had to tell them. That feeling – of shared concern and love – ended when Ruku left for Chotanagpur, after a brief visit to Calcutta this time round. Chitra and Arun threw broad hints Phalgun visited too often and without rhyme or reason. He went about with

Rukmini whenever and wherever he pleased. It simply didn't suit their style.

All this time Chitra hadn't once mentioned the girls marriage. Now she repeated, "One has to think about it – after all the girl can't be married off to just anybody?" Proposals for marriage started to arrive, especially from those successful types, who had done well in studies and in jobs. Phalgun had somehow scraped through with a M.A., although he was late in starting. His evenings were taken up by the Calcutta School of Music. People at large didn't enjoy western classical musical; all they got to hear was the version used as background music in films. Phalgun had no taste for such music. He sat at home and composed his own kind of music, took down notations and gave his creations all kinds of titles: Sunlight, the waning of the moon, the flaming halo etc., He had an intense desire, for the past two months, to daub the walls of his house with forms of his musical imagination. He kept on changing the colour of the walls. He loved to walk down the street and reach the house of a person in the city and play him a tune on his violin. That person lived in Bishop Lefroy Road. Phalgun and Ruku had often stood on the street in front of his house and watched the old ceiling fan slowly revolve in his sitting room. He was one of world's busiest of men. He sketched morning and night resting on a hugh arm chair with his feet up on a wooden footstool. Phalgun sat in a corner and played him his own compositions while the person was thus engaged. No word was spoken but Phalgun could sense his music had plumbed the depths of an animated stream where there was a play of light and shadow. Manikda would get up and unlatch the front door and ask him gently to wait when it was time for Phalgun to leave. His grave and sonorous voice would reverberate in the diffused light of the staircase.

There was one other person besides to whom Phalgun went, although he didn't dare intrude on the person's privacy. He was a professional through and through, rich and smart and had style. He stayed at Gurusaday Dutta Road – his name was M. Bhaskar. Although Bhaskar came from Andhra Pradesh his family had lived in Calcutta for three generations and dug their roots in the city. He played western classical music on the violin and mesmerized everyone with his extraordinary skills. He spent half the year in the USA and travelled homewards stopping in Paris, Italy and Turkey. Amiyada carried his messages to Phalgun. Bhaskar had heard a rendering of Phalgun's composition – A Halo of Flame – on an ordinary cassette and had turned grave; a deep line was etched on his forehead. He could recognise immediately what was genuine – the real stuff – like the goldsmith does the real gold. He hadn't come across such a combination of emotion and intelligence in a decade and a half. Perhaps no one had.

Phalgun hadn't mentioned a word about all this to his mother. She didn't even know when Amiyada had come and taken away the cassette. Phalgun felt bad about parting with the original – the person to whom it was dedicated hadn't heard it even once. Amiyada, however, couldn't be persuaded otherwise. Uma came home to find Bhaskar's Mercedes slowly taking the bend of their narrow alley. Her son wasn't in. The driver grew restless – he wouldn't wait for more than ten minutes – his master would miss his Delhi flight. Phalgun was nowhere to be seen.

When he was back the car had already left. Mritunjoy hadn't been in a good shape. The chest X Ray revealed white nebules on his left lung; he was suffering from an acute attack of pneumonitis. Mritunjoy had been running a temperature for the past few days, coughing and having headaches. He was almost unconscious the night before. Phalgun got the news from a boy next door. Mritunjoy managed, somehow, to give him his address. He could barely speak. The local doctor advised immediate hospitalization; he could look around for a nursing home if required. All this made Phalgun feel terribly confused. He recalled how another person, he knew in the area, had to sell off his land in order to admit his mother to a nursing home, how that person had to leave a gold chain at the reception counter as security so that his mother was taken in. The bill for ten days came to thirty two thousand rupees – doctors always went for such nursing homes! How could Phalgun decide what should be done with Mritunjoy? He had consulted no one and hadn't got hold of any money.

Mritunjoy had no relatives living at Calcutta, his old widower uncle stayed near Burrabazar. He simply refused to go to a nursing home, got agitated and said he wouldn't –not in this life. Phalgun calmed him down with great difficulty by giving him a dose of medicine prescribed by a doctor. He wiped his forehead with wads of cotton soaked in water and eau-de-cologne. His bed looked dirty; his quilt was tattered and torn and without a cover. A heap of unwashed clothes were piled on top of the clothes rack. The water pitcher kept in one corner of the room didn't have a lid. Unscrubbed utensils lay abandoned on the kitchen floor – a picture of graceless poverty! Phalgun took all this to heart as he gazed around the room. Was this the same man who had placed the flute on his hands? Mritunjoy had got both Ruku and him mad with music, playing on the flute on so many moon-flooded nights and stormy spring evenings! Some days they felt sorrowful, on other days as if they were breathing in the fragrance of the flowers of the Elysium, scattered all over the cloud-laden evening sky. Was this foul smelling man, with a stubbly chin, the same who had woven a magical spell around their lives?

Mritunjoy wasn't married; perhaps he hadn't the money. He earned so little and so irregularly that he found it difficult to see himself through the month. Ten out of fifteen pupils who came to him for a fortnight dropped out during the exam season. The five who stayed on were those whom the goddess Saraswati had shown the door. When he was in Class IX, finding Mritunjoy alone, Phalgun had gathered enough courage to ask him how he managed. Mritunjoy's voice was hoarse with cold, he made a hissing sound when he spoke. It was strange how strong and clear his voice sounded when he sang! One had to hear him in order to believe. He always smiled with a leftward twist to his lips: an expression of sarcasm. This time too he gave a twisted smile and said, "Why? Won't you all take care of me if anything happens – you all are my children, dear" "Ofcourse ..." Phalgun nodded his head shyly.

Phalgun saw a fat white cat perched on the boundary wall as soon as he came out of the place. There was nothing inside Mritunjoy's room, nothing except some last night's left-over milk. Phalgun had already placed a cover in case ... He realised that one wave of the cat's tail would send the cover rolling on the floor. He re-entered the room and placed a heavy stone mortar on its top. Mritunjoy lay as before with wads of wet cotton on his forehead. He kept his two hands folded on his chest and looked as if he was asleep. Although Phalgun walked without a sound he opened his eyes wide and asked, "You haven't gone as yet?"

"I was about to leave ... saw the cat on the boundary wall – the milk ..." "Cat!" Mritunjoy looked tired. He shut his eyes and mumbled what didn't make any sense to Phalgun. "Don't light the funeral pyre – I don't believe in all that. I'd have asked you to – had I any faith. Clean me properly, I haven't bathed for so many days!"

Phalgun lowered his face and ran his fingers through Mritunjoy's dusty hair and tried to bring them back into some shape. He said softly, "You musn't speak this way, Mastarmashai, you musn't – never think like this either. I have to be at home because I came without telling Ma. I'll be back in the afternoon. Sleep quietly if you can and shut the door behind me." Mritunjoy didn't respond, but his lips moved in silence; he gave the old twisted smile. What could a thief find in his decrepit house was probably what the smile meant. Phalgun had just placed a foot outside the threshold when he heard a frail voice, "You must take care of my flutes, the harmonium ..."

The driver had left the place, much vexed by the time Phalgun got back. Uma had a pan of vegetables on the stove.

"Why were you so late getting back?" she asked." You went out without having your morning cup of tea. Bhaskar's man had to leave – I entreated him to wait so many times but he wouldn't – said there was some important work – you know what a worrier I am!" In his imagination Phalgun could see impression of the tyre of the foreign car on their muddy lane; they seem to get fainter and fainter and finally fade away. The high flying moment for Phalgun had come and gone. He had missed the bus.

Now Phalgun had to run and implore Bhaskar to include him in his group else his massive ego would be hurt and Phalgun dropped from the tour. His name would also get cut off from the fellowship list and be rcplaced by some one else's. Phalgun frowned at the thought. He had been preparing to take a bath, putting aside the clothes he had on for washing. He oiled his thick hair and gave himself a look over in the bathroom mirror – the frown had vanished, his old face with a faint smile hovering over his lips looked back at him. He called out to his mother to prepare the rice, wondering whether he needed a shave. "I'll have to go to Mastarmashai's after I've eaten, Ma,"

"Who? Mritunjoy? What's the matter with him?"

"He's terribly ill with pneumonia. the doctor says ..."

Uma grew apprehensive, "Do we have to admit him to a hospital?"

"I don't know – I'll decide after I've had another look at him."

Uma had been cleaning the rice. She bit her lips. The veins on her cheeks were swollen to the point of bursting. Uma wasn't given to any display of emotion. No one had ever seen her cry. But today her aching body, imbecility of the gurseller, Chitra's insults all seemed to close in on her. She understood her son better than he did himself. Mritunjoy was ill – the boy won't move from his side. He was like that – holding on to something or someone he cared about till the last, with no thought for himself. Bhaskar had offered him his one big chance in life. Her face would have been saved, she would have been released from slander that her son was a good for nothing. But she couldn't tell Phalgun anything, he was, so to speak, the ground under her feet. Phalgun would look at her with his visibly pained starry eyes if she now suggested that he go immediately to Bhaskar's office, find out what he could still do and shelve the problem of looking after Mritunjoy till the evening. Phalgun would do exactly what he thought he should, that was his won't.

There was absolutely no point in telling him anything – none at all. It would create an unnecessary misunderstanding between themselves. Uma was on the verge of tears. Must she alone bear up under all kinds of strain in order to remain true to her own conscience? The walls of the room, the floor the calendar all became blurred in her vision. They suddenly cleared up and stood in their fixed and proper places as she had one look at her boy coming out of his bath with soulful eyes, free of glasses and the thick uncombed hair. She found herself at peace with the world. The boy had been Ananda's greatest gift to her, the source of joy in her life. She had never taken him to task leave alone spanking him. She had taken the boy up quietly and had held him close to her chest while the body of her husband was carried to the burning ghat. It was how she held him still, not once putting him down.

"Do whatever you feel like ... I won't say a word." Uma muttered to herself, not realising that Phalgun had heard what she said.

"Don't say anything more, Ma, It's alright." Phalgun came near her and began to wipe her moisture covered glasses with his undershirt.

Deep forests lay to the north of Duddhawa Block for the most part. Knobbly hills pocked out of the plateau and made for no particular direction. Prickly bushes grew on crevices along the hill slopes as well on their edges. Few people lived in the place. The little waterfall that ran down, flowed like a primitive canal here and there on the plains. Deers, wolves and leopards had made the place their home. The silent face of the sky was overwhelmed by the cries of thousands of birds. There were no proper roads or electricity in the area. Diagrams about construction of bridges over the river lay gathering dust in the district office. The place belonged to the Mundas and the Oram tribes, yet those people had no voice in the country's politics. Why would the government bother? A boy called Thomas Minz came to call on Ruku from a village in the highlands. He came with a petition filled wtih so many signatures – big scrawls, but more than often purple smudges of thumb impressions.

Strange situation that. And Bhalugaria was the headquarters of the panchayat, no less.

About thirty wells had been dug in six or seven of its villages – all lying half-finished, none complete. At places there were only dug holes, at other, only half the well was laid with stone. Work had begun at the end of the monsoon season and at the advent of autumn with funds allotted for development of the Adivasis. Money just stopped coming after the first round of work; construction came to a stop. People here were the poor peasants, the small or marginals tribals. They had no money of their own to fund the projects. Bhalugaria was situated at a considerable distance from the Block office yet people came to Duddhawa on foot or on the bus several times week. They came only to be told that they had not prepared their vouchers accurately; some times neither the accountant or the cashier were to be found. They had to go back emptyhanded without receiving money they were to be given in instalments. Now on top of it all the government officials were on strike!

It the wells didn't get dug now surely whatever remained would collapse especially if there were unexpected rains. No contractors had been appointed to oversee the planned project. How could people travel such distances each time only in order to collect money? Thomas Minz arrived at Duddhawa, walking twenty-six kilometers. His lissom body, tall as a sal tree, showed no signs of fatigue. Ruku knew the people assembled on the veranda had come there walking all the way from distant villages; the old among them must have suffered doubly because of the winter cold. But they were more than willing to spend whole nights in the chilly veranda, covering themselves tightly with a thin cloth of cotton in the hope that the next day they would receive pensions earmarked for the old and the widows.

The strike had ended a few days ago and Ruku managed to get Nareshbabu, the cashier and others to come to Bhalugaria with money – loads of it – account books and registers. An extraordinary mission. The mountain had indeed come to Mohamet! The wells were measured – one by one – vouchers made, money disbursed – all staying in one place. Ruku had spent the whole day giving the instalment money, bringing her office, so to speak, to the village. Though Nareshbabu had grumbled at the beginning he too conceded at the end, there was no rule in the book to prevent them from carrying on their work thus.

After a whole days work it was time for rest. The secluded villages did not provide adequate facilitities for that. While some went to sleep in the panchayat building Ruku stayed as the guest of the priest of Bhalugaria church. The father had come to the place from Ranchi; he was quiet and polite. He arranged Ruku to stay at a newly white-washed guestroom adjoining his house. The place was spick and span. The few pieces of furniture looked as if they were taken good care of and there was a clean old mosquito net. Incense was kept burning in one corner of the room. Ruku lay stretched on her stomach after she had had her dinner, washed and changed. After the flurry of activity and intense conversation throughout the day she was for the first time alone.

Phalgun's letter had been weighing down her conscience like a heavy stone. An unopened and unread letter which had reached her in the morning, carrying her office address. Perhaps some person had given it to Gulluram chawkidar. She had hesitated to read the letter while travelling and had carried it about her as it was. Night's darkness reigned out of doors. The moon had already climbed to the top of the mountains. The moonlight exuded the intoxicating jungle smell – the wild fragrance of the sunburnt *Mohul* and *Palash* trees. Colours of leaves – new, old and fallen – created a dazzle; the songs of night birds cast a magical spell. Ruku buried her face deep into the letter and lay for a while – she was afraid to read it. When the fear passed she read it over and over again as hours passed.

Ruku 5th February, Calcutta

I came home a little while ago with so many old flutes, of all sizes and shapes – only an harmonium got left behind. I'll have to fetch it tomorrow. I hadn't promised Mastarmashi anything but I feel it was the last thing he probably wanted me to.

Mritunjoy, Sir, left us early morning today – Saraswati puja day. Ma performed the ghat puja at home while I stayed out the entire time. I collected the flutes from his house on my way back from the burning ghat. Ma or Chitramashi never allowed me to play the flute but you know how, time and again, I had played a tune on it secretly while you sat by my side. Mastarmashi guided me to the world of music. This mundane earth had held out no attraction for me since then. You of course are my sole riches – but you are not entirely of this earth, you are also some kind of a fantasy – like the earth rising from the depths, if that is what one might see with feet firmly planted on the moon!

I have got into this habit – talking to you at nights. I indulge in a ten-minute soliloquy before I go to bed. Now I am worried I may not be able to get out of the habit and go on babbling even though you might be sleeping by my side!

I know I won't sleep tonight – actually I have a terrible fear; fear of a ugly unredeemed end to life. I have seen clearly how those who have no proper livelihood, who don't manage to become rich overnight, have undignified death, in spite of their talent or genius. I see myself as one of them —

I had to take Mastarmashai to the hospital the evening before last; I couldn't trace any relatives save a distant uncle. I couldn't muster courage to admit him to a nursing home, my dear. No matter how noble I appear it's all because my mother is so gutsy. I got hold of Ashok Kundu, the house staff at the medical college – he lives in the neighbourhood, remember – and got Mastarmashi admitted to the hospital. I didn't spend a penny, got the death certficate in the bargain. But no one took care of poor Mastarmashai. A young doctor had come in the morning and examined him with the stethescope. I wasn't in the hospital then. The nurse changed the saline drip and then there was a big rush to get oxygen. I sat out the night on a stool and watched the life of a free-bed patient come to an end. Who knows whether he would have lived had I borrowed money and taken him to a nursing home. Perhaps he would have died all the same. I sit and make all kinds of wild guesses –

I remain happy in spite of all my fears, happy because I have you. Mastarmashi had no one, no one to call his own. I also think that I wouldn't have had a life full of music if we hadn't grown up together, if I hadn't seen you morning and night. Perhaps then I'd have hunted around for jobs after my graduation, if not earlier. Perhaps I'd have tired myself out by now. But as I saw you everyday a symphony of colours covered my entire being! It hid me like the flowery creeper does the split, dried up bark of a tree. My music sheltered me from the cruel discerning gaze of society, hid my worthless self while I gazed at the stars and moved towards my morrow under the cover of a song!

You know best how Chitramashi had tried to make me study, coaxing and cajoling me, and making me completely beholden to her by feeding me such delicious meals. Although my mother never took me to task for my laziness she would always hold you up as a bright example in front of my eyes. 'Can't you become like her?" she would say. Now Chitramashi would rather I didn't go over to your house; she looks worried when I do. I have nothing to distinguish myself, no achievements or status in society. There is no place for me in your home. But

I'm always surprised at people's expectations of me. Why must I be like you? You always did well in studies, was excellent in debates, came first in literary composition. It's wonderful for me that you managed to reach for the moon leaving me free to do what others don't consider worthwhile.

Ma suffers because of this – she thinks Chitramashi and Arun Mesho have changed towards us, especially after you came and went, not so long ago. Now they are displeased to see me. They discuss their plans for your future in front of Ma which she finds hard to accept. I've told Ma I'm looking for a job ... will get one soon enough. There's a new research center in Jodhpur Park. It publishes a journal. I may become its assistant editor. Its a quiet place with nothing to hassle one.

The shelves are lined with books. You'll like the place. I also have my music.

I think I've lost the chance Bhaskar gave me. I couldn't go to him because of Mritunjoy Sir's illness. I could've travelled to the USA for six months, got a fellowship to go to a university if Bhaskar had put in a word. He has done many that favour. But I'm not unhappy about it. What'll I do going so far away from you or home? I doubt I'd have the urge to play music, muffled in an overcoat from head to toe. I am fairly happy as I am. I sit facing my favourite window every evening. I play the violin without stop untill all the stars come out in the sky. I haven't once turned my gaze away from *that* window. I see your face there, the twinkle in your eyes, even the dimple on your cheeks – all in that window frame whether my eyes are open or shut.

Sometimes I think of that mango tree in Hazaribagh, aglow with fireflies. I can imagine clearly all the non-descript rivers about which you write. I see you – cooking late at night in the kitchen blackened by soot and smoke – you thrusting the wet wood into the stove while the foliage of the wild tamarind tree makes shadowy lace-like patterns on your back.

I now compose with you on my mind. I place you in different scenes in my imagination. I give my compositions many titles ... You have broken out of that little window frame, you have spread your wings into the sky but like the seed, buried in earth, you're still a part of me. Chitramashi, Mesho or Ma cannot make you out – they cry, they sulk, they see you differently. But I haven't lost you because I've no separate memory of getting you. You were a part of my consciousness from the moment I became aware. You were not above me or below me but inseparable from my being. I have known nothing else but you.

You sit with pen and paper and I wait eagerly to see what you have written. You go to school and I look for you to get back so that I can see you again. You fall down and bruise your knees I wonder when the wound will heal and your leg become the same as before. Tell me, if a boy thinks like this from the age of eleven or twelve and without rhyme or reason what could he have left? He doesn't enjoy solving mathematical problems, doesn't want to win a game of cricket as you are the only source of happiness in his life. This kind of happiness doesn't make me miss you when you are not here. I sit mesmerized by the window frame. Now tell me is it any wonder Chitramashi is so annoyed with me or – that she gets exasperated?

I want to tell you about my new composition for you – a wonderful piece! I have just finished composing it. Amiyada turned up and took the cassette away and I'm a bit annoyed. The music is out of this world! I have never attempted anything like this earlier.

In the opening notes you are a little butterfly then you grow into a dense *Baobab* tree and the entire world seeks your shelter. You leave behind the familiar, pot-holed, gulmohar covered road and sit rubbing your shoulders against the mountains. A breeze from the river wafts you away; multicoloured butterflies ring around you in the almond and green hued earth. I witness the scene standing at a distance. I see a bluish halo and can't make out whether it's light or fire. Then the whole scene dissolves, gets smaller and smaller within me till nothing is left except for a dim light at the end of a long tunnel. Do you think I could make this music for anyone else but you or play it to others? I'll make you listen to it when you are back. Better still I'll go to you myself and play it for you. I am reluctant to leave mother alone and go anywhere at all. Don't be angry. I haven't stopped relying on Chitramashi!

Reading your letter about the delivery of potatoes I have some idea about the back-breaking work you have to do. You seem to be in another world altogether, one which has different set of norms. But I have no worry about my little bird – no one can teach her a lesson by piling her with work. I worry that you don't eat properly and that you don't take care how you look, that you might catch chill while returning from work during night as the cold wind blows in through the tattered hood of the jeep. You have the habit of misplacing your comb – take care, your hair will be in knots if you don't comb your hair out every night.

I haven't called your 'my Ruku' – intentionally. I try to comprehend a situation where our little bird is hopping over leaves and branches of a big, big tree. So many people are coming to you – so many events are taking place around you every day. You have left us and glided into the wide world. It's good to cultivate this kind of stoicism so that I can see myself with some sense of objectivity. But this cultivated indifference towards you is but momentary. Sooner or later I will resume my old attitude. Don't be cross.

I read your published poems over and over again. I don't regret you are not able to write like before. Your poems are your signature – I've known that all along. History will not record your future achievements. These poems will last like my musical creations, these you will leave behind for posterity. Some one else will play my music sitting next to a flame in the darkened world. The essence of a person's soul is discovered in the soul of another. One goes through life in its search. We have found that within ourselves. Now all we have to do is to get along with our lives.

The night is about to come to an end. Birds are beginning to stir. Night time is always a time of unknown fears and strange sounds, when we feel danger lurking. The birds are awake ere the day has begun; they are the harbingers of another new day in our lives. Rays from the sun are gradually lightning up the bluish purple hat of the sky. Mastarmashi has gone so far away. Last night I was going mad trying to get hold of people who might tell me whether he was still alive, making a commotion in the somnolent hospital. His flutes are lying on my table, but the piper has left us with the morning light and scattered himself all over the sky. I exult in the wondrous thing called life. I feel its joy and its miracle. I have a sense of pride about its potential to set us free.

My dear Ruku, perhaps I've never told you about my love for you. But how can I describe what I think or feel as love? It's like an ocean filling up the corners of the earth where the sun goes down in bits and pieces and which is ruffled by the wings of the trafficking birds. I grew up ensconced in your self, no one else's shadow was cast over my existence. We are not two individual human beings. We are one and the same. I cannot lose you – ever. And I don't have to measure up to you in terms of society. It's not important for me to know now where you are or when and how you'll come back – to us. People will taunt you about me and raise doubts about my worth but one day that game of tipping the scales will end, leaving us both in a state of peace and happiness. Those who we bring into this world will remain forever young, like us. They will not be impeded by the constant need to succeed.

Music has a message for me – I am so immersed in it! If I utter it you may think its silly, trivial. It's this: If one doesn't love being simply alive then he cannot fill up the emptiness within, no matter how much he tries to. I've been spared the stultifying effect of running after worldly success. I enjoy the sheer fact of being alive. I like to see your sleepy face in the morning, do something frivolous like procuring paper and stamps for you or heating up your bathwater.

I know that the great universe of men will beckon you to it all the time, unfold important events to your eyes, thrill you to bits but you'll come back to me – pulled by the lure of sheer happiness!. I'll leave the world placing my violin in your hands. I won't have to scout the skies to find someone to carry on my creative pursuits. Mritunjoy Sir had to ... so that his flutes could find a resting place.

The star of my eyes, the ocean of my dreams now go to sleep, I know you'll read this letter before Morpheus takes over.

Yours only, Phalgun.

A man, seemingly old, had come and gone back thrice, bringing her a cup of tea. Ruku was deep in sleep, she hadn't opened the door. Finally, Father himself came, clattering his sandals and knocked.

By the time they returned the evening had folded in. They washed, had some tea and bread and went over to another village. Even though Bhalugaria was the panchayat headquarter, some of its members lived in Asantanr. The jeep made a rattling sound as it moved. Asan tanr – does it mean the place was full of *Asan* trees once? Now it looked like any other village –

rundown, uneven and a mixture of green and brown. Ruku noticed huge *sal* trees, the *palash* was in flower. The blossoms of *shimul* trees were rolling on the dusty earth. At places wild thickets sprung from the bowels of the earth where old soil conservation tanks existed, at other the crumbled-down walls of a school building. She had to inspect everything. Funds were scarce, but had to be spent wherever it was necessary.

Most of the officers on extension didn't want to travel to the interior. They would prefer to use up all the funds for developing the five mile region surrounding the Block Headquarters. There were no proper roads for miles; the jeep got back bumping and switching sides. Another five miles to go before they could hit the panchayat road, not so bumpy although it wasn't tarred.

Thomas Minz led the way as driver Kishan had no clue about the area. He had on an old pair of trousers, a dirty banian and torn canvas shoes. He leapt like a jungle deer in front of the jeep as it went along. He didn't look like a human being at all but some unearthly creature.

Thomas wouldn't leave them even after they had reached the tarred road. Finally, scolded by Ruku, he stepped aside and stood at one side of the road, wiping off perspiration from his arms with a big smile on his face.

The road took a bend further on. When Ruku looked back she saw Thomas still stationary, under a barren *shimul* tree. He had a fifteen mile romp ahead of him – to return home – to hunger and darkness.

Seven

The final chapter of the training programme was about to commence under the cloudscapes of Mussoorie in early spring. Girls and boys were already back from the districts; a year had gone by. So many things had changed over the time while much remained the same. Standing on the wooden balcony of the Ladies' Block one could see still the early morning sun dazzle the long line of the snow topped mountains and in the front a sequence of little peaks, blue and green, hide colourful images within their folds, the pine trees bathed in sunlight. It hardly rained now, although the weather was breezy and the lawns decked with rows of flowers of all description in bloom. Nature had emptied out all its riches to welcome back the prodigals! Agamchand, Sukhchand and Sishram were bustling about the place – bringing the tea, ironing clothes or fetching food from mess. The familiar boys and girls with whom they had established friendship were back. They uttered "Good morning" or "Ram, Ramji"when they came across them on the streets.

Ruku wasn't given her old room, she had one in the corner of the first floor now. She couldn't take her eyes away from the tableland ready with the colours of spring or the hills bordering its three sides. A year was not such a long time after all, but people become so different once out of sight. Those who felt they hadn't changed looked sad if others gazed at them with amazement. Sudev Kapur hadn't bothered to step into the balcony to find out why the girl called Mohini had to be rushed to the hospital, creating such commotion in the campus, one beautiful spring night. 'Akashdeep', reserved for the honeymooning couples, though situated beyond campus gates, was not cut off from the din and clamour of men and traffic.

Sudev had opened his eyes only once and had gone back to sleep. His gold-bangled, newly-wed wife had her arms nestling close to his chin. Sudev's parents lost no time after he completed his training to find a girl – the second daughter of the chief engineer – with a lot of gold, a car and a flat and get him married according to the Hindu rites. The thought of a mature daughter-in-law, from a different state, was not some thing they could take. Who was there to control her? She not only held a job but was a dancer as well – an Orissi dancer! Hardly likely to be docile. Besides she would have come to them empty-handed – would the son have demanded a thing when marrying for love? And who could tell if a girl from another community wouldn't have turned them out of their home. Purnima was better in every respect. She was pretty, quiet, aware of social norms; a younger daughter of an extremely rich parents. Thank goodness, their son concurred though he had looked grumpy. The parents didn't wait but married him off on the first auspicious phase of the moon during the month of *Ashar*.

Mohini and Sudev hadn't been getting along for some months. Sudev seemed to be indifferent; his letters were brief and curt. Mohini had thought of going over to his place and clearing up the misunderstanding when Aradhana, from the next district, rang her up and said, "What's up Mohini ... didn't you know Sudev is about to marry?"

Mohini was stunned. Broken-hearted, she cried continuously for several days. Officers in the settlement camp didn't know what to do with her. She returned to the campus without a word. How could Sudev, who was loathed to stay a minute away from her, forget her completely now? Behave as if she didn't exist? Couldn't they have remained friends even though he was married? Mohini was without any hope; she kept smoking like a chimney while cigarette stubs continued to pile up on the ash tray. She could be found lying in a distraught state with a night dress on in the afternoons when classes were on in full swing. The counsellor sent for her, the deputy director dispatatched memos: Mohini remained unmoved. Kusum came wearing a purple chiffon saree and carrying a box of *Benarasi zarda.* Kusum had waist-length flowing golden hair, a figure to envy and a husky voice to boot. She gave her loads of advice. "Why break down so easily, silly girl ... there are many men like Sudev waiting in the wings. Look at me – I broke off my engagement to Ashok, have got rid of Raj, now Gaurav is restless to marry me. Men are meant to be replaced, dear! Come on, get up, take a bite of the *zardapan.*" By then, Mohini's large black eyes were brimming with tears.

The floodgates actually opened on the night of the 'welcome dinner'. Mohini was dressed to kill in Sudev's favourite blue *sambalpuri* saree, hoping she would get the chance to talk to him. Surely he would find some excuse to leave his wife behind, for her to gossip with other new brides, and come to the balcony. They had stood there together so many nights after dinner, under the dim light and hadn't stirred until the bearer had chased them away so that he could lock the door. The Himalayas and dense forests covering the valley appears behind the balcony of wrought-iron railings in the light of day. But at night there is only darkness, the beam of light from the lamp post, smell of woods and a fresh cool breeze brushing the cheeks. Sudev had pulled an unaware Mohini into the balcony and kissed her deeply, on her cheeks, neck and lips – before they had left for their village visit. Then there was no turning back – it became a craze with them; Mohini, herself, took him there. They had laughed, joked and said so many things to each other about their one year separation. How quickly Sudev had forgotten all that! He hadn't come and spoken a word leave alone ask her for her forgiveness. Don't people introduce their wives to their erstwhile girlfriends?

Women and men were chatting after dinner, sitting scattered on sofas. Some kept standing. A slow-stepped dancing had begun. Mohini stood alone in the dark veranda, her eyes fixed on Sudev. Familiar features – the same nose, chin and hairstyle – yet a totally strange face. Was he the same Sudev who had sat resting his chin on her knees and wouldn't let her go if she wanted to get up? The same man who had embarassed her by turning up at the Ladies' Block at all odd hours? What if she now went and revealed all that to the stupid wife of his, told her everything about their past?

Sudev carefully picked a toothpick from the silver tray, helped himself to the fennel seeds and gave some to his wife. He brought out his packet of cigarettes and matches. Mohini stared steadily at him. Sudev gave a slight laugh and shook his head when someone tapped his shoulders; he then put his arm casually around his wife's waist and tip-toed to his room across the blue-carpeted floor. One minute he was there, the next he was gone. When the two melted into the darkness Mohini muttered to herself, "Men are meant to be replaced", the words of Kusum. By then, unknown to her, her blouse had got soaked with tears streaming down her cheeks.

Steps were taken quickly otherwise it wouldn't have been possible to arrange for the stomach wash. A pale, dark-looking Mohini returned to the campus after a ten-day stay at the hospital. This Mohini didn't bear the faintest resemblance to the old Mohini Misra save for the nose. Her lips were contorted, she spoke with a hoarse voice, didn't talk or smoke. In class, she took down notes with her head lowered; in her room in the afternoons she practised Orissi dance in front of the mirror with jingling anklets tied to her infirm feet. But she spoke out gaily saying, "How are you," to Sudev if their paths crossed. Those were the moments her face glowed. She looked severe and full of despair the minute Sudev was out of sight. Mohini was not the same person anymore; she had changed but not in the way Sudev had.

Sunila Oram was still the same. She was Mohini's room mate but chose to stay out of her sight these days. She turned in only when she felt she had to go to bed. It was she who had noticed phials of sleeping tablets lying on the table and on the floor. Mohini wouldn't have been taken to the hospital in time if Sunila hadn't rung Dr. Bosu immediately. Now she was not sure whether Mohini was angry with her or grateful to her for what she did. She thought it best to make herself scarce when Mohini was back from the hospital.

Sunila would walk over to room number seventy eight as soon as classes ended and Kishnu darwan would quickly open the room for her. Swaruplall had stayed in that small green attic room; it hadn't been given to anyone this term for some unknown reason. Sunila had free access to the place – it was a small gift she deserved. The riding ground below was visible from one of its windows, the road toiling up and the long line of substantial deodar trees as well. Sunila and Swarup had walked back to the campus along this path in the dark, before they had to leave for the 'village visit'. Sounds of that laughter-filled evening still rang in her ears.

The room was now empty. The authorities had packed and sent the few things Swarup possessed to Hoshiarpur. A bare bed, a dressing table with a tarnished mirror, a couple of chairs positioned opposite each other, were all there was. Sunila started opening the drawers of the book shelf; pieces of paper lay there – paper cuttings, typed class notes with Swarup's handwritten comments along the margin. Sunila gathered them together with loving care. Bits of paper, cut out in the shape of stamps, with her name Sunila, repeatedly written lay in the bottom drawer. Childish Swarup! Now they were stuck and she couldn't scratch them out with her nails. Her eyes got misty trying to retrieve them. How her life had changed only because of that one person who was no longer. They had wanted ordinary things out of life – to stay together – but even that had remained unfulfilled. It had been better, perhaps, if Swarup had rejected her and married someone else. She could have continued to see him as she went about her normal activities. But no, she would never take her life as Mohini had tried to.

Sunila Oram was a different person when she trotted down the stairs and left the precincts of the Ladies' Block. With her hair brushed back and made into a tight bun (not a straggely strand on her forehead or shoulders), and saree in place, fastened by a shoulder broach, Sunila was smiling constantly, reaching out her hands to the needy. All the children living in the huts knew her as they knew Dr. Bosu. The mothers of the children worked as coolies carrying stones across the mountains or as servants in large bungalows. The children suffered from eyes-sores, all kinds of skin ailments, colds and coughs. Caught up in the atttractive games especially arranged for them in the campus they were reluctant to go back to their homes. Professor Shyamakanta Sinha was in charge of social development projects; his work lightened considerably when Ruku and Sunila made regular visits.

Classes continued to be held. They had to sit for a minor exam, make seminar presentations, write long essays, do research in the Library's reference room. Hardly a couple of months left for all of this to come to an end. Then the bell would ring – not for holidays but work, in the real sense of the term. They would be closing shop and entering the world – leaving for their first posting, earning their living.

The tarred road, that rubbed against the mountains, stretched from the arched gate to the market corner. It reached the Mall and then extended way beyond it. A rather long road, but pleasant to walk with mountains displaying the many coloured rocks on one side. The wild flowers and the sun-parched earth gave off a strong smell. Down below, beyond the railings, lay the valley with huts nestling on the inclines of the hills, and then there was such feast for the eyes – the greens and the blues – the bluish-green peaks jutting out of the clouds. Ruku never felt tired walking along this way in company. All the wonderful colours were absent during night, substituted by rows of lamps fixed in their places throwing light. That too had a beauty of its own. Ruku had taken in the wondrous phenomenon when she covered the route in the company of men. She had wanted to have her fill of the radiating beauty of the sky and the mountains; she knew it would be lost to her forever as soon as she was back on the plains.

Shops sprung up where the road took a corner turn: a studio which rented out cameras, a cheap restaurant, a coffee joint and an expensive hotel, which had a dance hall with coloured lamps on the first floor. Hillfolk sat on roadsides and sold woollies, beads and trinkets. Further down were the falling levels of the valley all along the mountain edge. There was nothing to beat the pleasure of a walk here on a sunny day. The town or the market didn't come to life on their own – waited expectantly for the commencement of the tourist season. The splendid display of merchandise was really for the outsiders. Big luxury buses from the plains stopped there. There were rickshaws and taxi stands to cater to people moving in the opposite direction. Cars were not allowed on the Mall. Men pulled rickshaws – four of them in the front and two pushing from behind – to carry the tourists on sight-seeing trips. The huge wooden box-like seats were difficult to climb in and out of even at the best of times. The sightseers, big and fat men and women, sat on them nervously looking up at the sky. It made Ruku laugh. Girls and boys from the campus walked all the way here, even went down to Dehradoon and took a cab straight back to the post office.

Ruku and Sonal came panting in and threw their bags full of shopping on the bed. They were perspiring after the brisk walk. A merrily prancing Kuldeep followed them from behind.

He had a bag on one hand, held a polythene packet of *gulab jamuns* and the famous *barfies* from the corner shop on the other. Standing on the threshold he shouted, "Get up you lazybones! Don't pretend illness. And now see – how one look at the *pantuas* makes him sit up straight! Poor *Bhabi*, her arms must have nearly dropped off carrying all the load!"

Navroj was stretched out on bed. He had been feeling achy and feverish since the morning; he had a thick sweater and pyjama on and was wrapped up in a light kulu shawl. He didn't raise his voice and said, "I had asked you to accompany your *Bhabi* knowing she is frail – what do you think? Must you only gaze at her feet?"The two still carried on their village parlance, joked and bantered in the fashion of rural folk although they spoke English mildly and politely when they sat in the campus lounge. They took off their masks when by themselves and indulged in rural punjabi capers.

Sonal puckered her brows. "Come on, sit up, see what all we've bought – no, no, stay till I give *Didi* a drink. She'd been complaining about feeling thirsty for a long time." Ruku had taken out the woollen shawl, a sweater, an ordinary wrap and bed sheets and had displayed them on the bed: all the stuff Sonal had gone crazy and bought. They cost quite a bit even though some items were cheaper here than at Jullunder or Chandigarh. But shopping at Mall was such fun! Sonal had been to Chandigarh only once when she was really tiny and couldn't remember a thing about the place. She hadn't as yet learnt that money was no object when it came to buying things. She was used to spending on *atta*, rice, sugar and kerosene oil and occasionally on clothes she would wear. Now that she was married there was no one to control her; with no village elders to frown down upon her she felt like a lark. Though she didn't have money to burn, she felt free and fearless as a wild peacock. Kuldeep had come out of the tiny kitchen carrying a plateful of sweets; he hadn't washed his hands. "My hands are licked clean!" He claimed.

One by one they all took a helping of the *pantuas*. Kuldeep struck his hand against his breast pocket and exclaimed, "Good heavens – where on earth have I left the parcel?"

"What parcel?" asked Sonal.

"Why the one you gave me to keep, remember? Ah, here it is ..."

Two tiny socks, a bonnet and a pair of mittens in pink and white! Nobody had an inkling when Kuldeep had bought them or where he had kept them hidden – clothes for a new born baby.

"I never bought these!" Sonal's face reddened in embarassment.

Navroj laughed loudly. Ruku was angry. "Why Kuldeep, you shouldn't have done that – I wouldn't have gone out with you had I known you're up to such tricks."

"Ok dear ok." Kuldeep found himself cornered. "Yes ... I bought them. But they'd come to use in a year and half's time."

Sonal gave an angry look and went in to prepare the tea.

A tiny kitchen with a few pots and pans and a kerosene stove. There were exactly two plates, one of which had to be washed up if there were three for dinner. A middle-sized bedroom with a double bed. Sonal's sarees, *salwar-kameez* were flung on the other rack without any order. Navroj's shirts and pants lay on top. The entire room reeked of unfamiliarity with domestic living. Two huge suitcases and a bedding were pushed underneath the bed. Navroj had married Sonal on his way back from the training camp. The wedding couldn't take place in the village, with the village elders remaining as adamant as before. They got married in the Durga temple in Simla. His father and uncle refused to see the bride when he took her to his ancestral home, but they spared her abuse.

His aunt laughed and wept and welcomed the bride by placing a necklace belonging to Navroj's mother around her neck. She asked after Sonal's mother over and over again – they had been childhood friends and now lived at the opposite ends of Himachal Pradesh. Navroj's aunt had news of her friend once in a while from people travelling to those regions. She knew about Sonal's mother's widowhood, Sonal growing up and going to school, her mother taking up a job with the panchayat.

His aunt had become a prisoner in Navroj's ancestral home ever since his mother died. She hadn't been happy about staying there but couldn't free herself of fetters of social convention and move out. Navroj started visiting Sonal at her behest. At that time he was little aware about the deep feelings Sonal had for him. The smile on her face – of those dreamy childhood days – was cruelly wiped off by the condemnation of the village heads. Navroj belonged to a lower caste; he was a Harijan. Did a pariah dog dare eat rice served in respectable households that Navroj could dream of marrying a brahmin virgin?

Today that dream had come true. Navroj's aunt was beside herself in joy. She put on the pot of rice, then took down a pan of oil lest it became too hot. Beneath it all there lurked a sneaking anxiety for her childhood friend. Suppose she was ostracised by the entire community, insulted and tortured? Navroj and Sonal had both advised her to leave the village if the situation became intolerable. Navroj was an adult now – not an unemployed student. He was a magistrate and had lots of friends scattered over several districts. He had become mentally and physically stronger. The village heads sensed the altered circumstances; they left Usha alone. She, on her part, didn't once think of abandoning her husband's home.

Rukmini was giving Navroj's room a look over while Sonal prepared the tea. Sonal and Navroj had known each other for so long yet they hadn't, it seemed, crossed the hurdle of strangeness. The room belied signs of their unease with each other. It was different in the village. Here – among a crowd of sophisticated men and women in the variegated atmosphere of a town – Sonal appeared lost and diffident. She clung to Rukmini whenever she took a single false step or uttered the wrong word. She worried about what she would wear, how she would put her hair up, what she would cook – these thoughts comprised her outlook on life. Her's was a small world.

A simple and innocent girl from the village Sonal didn't have a clue about Navroj's feelings for Rukmini or the storm that had raged within him before he married her. But both Navroj and Rukmini hadn't forgotten all that. Ruku could, in her ease and naturalness, overcome her hesitations and establish a deep friendship with Sonal; Navroj still felt awkward.

His face reddened when he came across Rukmini. Till yesterday he had felt a thrill, enough to take his breath away, at her presence. He had dreamt of spending days and nights with her. How could he then accept her moving about freely in his own household? He felt he was a lone train that had got derailed in the deep of night – he hadn't as yet hardened to the idea he would have to keep his feelings in check.

Navroj had to be cruel to himself, use moral arguments, in order to bring his emotions under control. He was only human after all. He had recovered his adolescent affection for Sonal when he visited her again after a gap of time; it was an affection comingled with concern for her safety and sympathy for her solitary existence. He had to reassure Usha – rescue mother and daughter from the cruel clutches of the village folk – without delay. He had achieved that much. But deep in his heart still flowed the stream of passion – like some molten lava inside a volcano – though he never let those feelings come to the surface. That's the way it was and would be – for months and years to come, possibly till he was dead.

Years would go by, Navroj get older and grayed by experience, his apple-like cheeks would get lined with age, but love, like the lava at the center of the earth, would become more condensed and strong. Bound by inner conscience Navroj never once tried to look up Rukmini even though he had to change planes in the very city where she lived. Those days following his marriage were for him like dress rehearsals for battles he would have to wage within himself in times to come.

Thank goodness Rukmini never guessed what lay behind his shyness. She had concluded that the conflictual chapter of her life had ended with her restoring Sonal to Navroj. Her heart was already filled with thoughts of Phalgun. She was ready to unfold her aesthetic wings and glide into the immense star-studded sky, breaking out of the silken cocoon of her existence. In her consciousness Navroj, Sonal, Kuldeep were unreal – all alike. While she had come and stood by them, laughed and extended to them her love, it was Phalgun who stirred her whole being like the full flowering gulmohar tree creating waves of shadow.

Then the day came when all was destroyed, everything went to rack and ruins, merging with rocks and stones: mansions like palaces, the pleasant lounge and the veranda, the large dinning hall frequented by men and women for over thirty years in this land of the clouds – all. Those men and women had left the signatures of their many thoughts there, had lost their hearts to each other – those memories vanished into thin air within a matter of seconds.

Ruku was suddenly awake at the middle of the night. She had gone to sleep rather late, around eleven. The campus was totally deserted by ten-thirty generally; only the soft footfalls on the blue carpeted wooden floor of the Ladies' Block could be heard. People slept in the huts. The mild breeze from the mountains stirred the leaves of the long line of deodar trees – one night during the month of *Chaitra*.

At a time like this the plateau of Chota Nagpur, abandoned

by Ruku, must have reddened with *palash*, and leafless *shimul* trees! Here there was only a drowsy stillness; one didn't even hear the flapping of night birds. Ruku couldn't recall what dreams she had been having; she was suddenly woken by the voices of women crying out loudly. Somehow it sounded like the howling of dogs floating out of the distant moon. She got up and sat on her bed, startled. Priya was asleep on the next cot, Priya Ranganathan.

Ruku moved quickly to the veranda and was stung by freezing cold outside.A coil of faint mist hung loosely around the body of deodar trees. People were running at great speed below ... who were they? A group of people came rushing up the stairs and forced open the mat door as she looked on. All headed for the Main Block. She heard shouts.

Putting on a sweater. Ruku went down the stairs. She didn't know what to think. Sunila was out with a torch with Kamaljit from Punjab following closely behind.They had hardly reached the end of the road that led to the Ladies' Block when they saw flames of fire blazing against the dark blue sky and the thick pile of a suffocating black smoke. The entire left portion of the entrance to the Main Block was burning furiously ... the other portion appeared hazy in all the smoke and flying ashes. It was impossible to breathe. Mess was located right below – in the basement. All the cooking was done there. Huge furnaces resembling wide open mouths of monsters were kept burning day and night. That's why the floor remained fire hot even during the winter cold. Provisions for six months – rice, *dal*, *rajma*, cornflakes and vegetables to last a week, dozens of eggs, tomatoes, potatoes and onions – were arranged on the shelves. Rare crokery, silverware and cutlery were stored in the cupboards. Rajinder, the president of mess committee, had come out into the open and was expressing loud regrets. Accountant Harish Lakhani hit at his own forehead in self-infliction. The torn jacket-clad old mess bearer kept running to and fro the smoke-filled room, holding the dinner sets close to his chest – it was all he could save from destruction.

"Stop them, please ... don't go there, you'll burn to death." Ruku and Kamaljit kept pulling at the rolled up sleeves of the singed, ash-covered jackets. In the din and noise, no one paid heed to what they said. Only Phaguram fixed a blank stare at Ruku. For him, fear of death and the fear of losing his job and starving to death was one and the same.

Water? Where was water ... anywhere? How could the fire be put out without a drop of it? Water – a scarce commodity in those mountainous regions even at the best of times. People living in the bustees didn't have enough to bathe or wash clothes. Water was also rationed in the hostels. Boys were seen running with water, stored in pails and jugs. But how could such a small quantity of it control the flame that had leapt into the sky and covered it? It would evaporate within seconds! Sparks, smoldering pieces of wood and stone from 'the house of wax' fell on Ruku and others.

They were forced to retreat.

The entire situation was beyond them. There was no water or fire brigrade. Every item in the Main Block fell victim to the relentless game of destruction by fire. The lounge burned furiously, with flames touching the ceiling of guest rooms above. Fire spread without interruption towards the GB Pant Block. There was nothing for Ruku and others to do but wait for it to end.

The entire campus was awake witnessing the destruction of their favourite building. The old men who waited on them stood like the barren, twisted old tree trunks; their eyes wide open. They must have wondered how they would earn bread in the midst of all the devastation.

Fire kept burning even the day after and a thick black smoke spiralled to the sky with dogged determination still a day later. Boys and girls tired and chilled to the bones returned to their own Blocks. On the way Ruku noticed Ramlall, standing like some stone statue, under the tinned roof of the office building – in the dark. His house was way down. One had to descend several steps and take a long walk to reach his little wooden hut with a tin roof.Ruku knew where he lived because she and Kuldeep had taken him food on a covered dish, when he was absent during their dinner party due to illness. Ramlall was late in receiving the news of the fire – details of the devastation hadn't penetrated the closed doors of his house below the valley. He had rushed when he heard. He couldn't save his favourite corner shop from the fiery onslaught. Ramlall had more than three hundred records, a record player and a microphone in his shop. Besides he sold cigarettes, chewing gum and chocolates. Nothing was spared. Rafi's soulful *Chawdhvi ki Chand* or Batalvi's ghazals – Kuldeep's favourite songs – would never again bellow from the charred remains of what was once a shop. Ramlall burst into tears when Ruku called out to him gently by name. Then he howled. People gathered and tried to reason with him. How could they help a person who had not only lost a shop but an emotional harbour?

The library was in the basement. A narrow soft, red carpeted, staircase wound its way there. It had no windows – the entire place was encased by glass through which, on a day when the air was free of moisture, one could see the rows of mountains, trees, huts and a play of light and shade in the hill foldings – as in a picture. Ruku had spent many melancholy days in the library, read quietly, taken out a Jibanananda Das volume from the shelf of Bengali books, in the hope she would find the key to the strange beauty of the hills in his poetry. Thousands of volumes precious manuscripts, complete sets of periodicals were all reduced to ashes. The fire was ignited by a short circuit of wire in the library, it had blazed its way up and spread wherever it was fed.

When the sun rose in the morning Ruku and others discovered that the valley had moved nearer, almost next door, leaping over the wreckage left by half-burnt GB Pant; the burnt-down pillars of the Main Block, ashes and burnt particles camouflaged the ground. The hollow below had turned even wider, large mouthed, displaying emptiness. The mountain suddenly fell from where they stood. Ruku was least prepared to see such phenomenon. She had enjoyed the sight of the snow-clad mountains from the safe distance of the veranda next to the blue carpeted lounge, and had felt happy. Others like Sudev and Mohini had exchanged their intimate confidences. The darkness of the veranda had captured and preserved the precious, private moments of so many lives. Now the sun and the wind roamed freely unhampered by those memories, No human edifice stood in the way of Nature's ceaseless motions.

Time had come for them to pack up and leave – the raging flames had disturbed equivalences between so many things. There was nothing to distinguish between the place where they sat down to eat and where they gathered for chats – now. The relief camp merged into the picnic ground. Breakfast was served below, lunch and dinners in batches in several hostels. After dinner *tête a tête* was totally abandoned. People returned to their rooms chewing fennel seeds and lumps of sugar. Class rooms didn't pose any space problems – these were always scattered over the place as on the camel's hump. But mistaking the new arrangements people often arrived late for class. The professors were too depressed to serve 'memos' to erring students. The chilly gaps in-between the mountains stared at the face as they moved around. Rubble was being crushed and removed by bull dozers and dump tracks – the ground was getting levelled and costs of new construction calculated. Nothing could make them get over the sense of a terrible loss.

The day arrived when they had to leave, go down to Dehradoon to take the bus to Delhi. Some travelled by train, others took cabs. Packing was complete during the wee hours of morning. Goodbyes were said – to those like Shishram without a roof over their heads, to the teachers at the post office, the gardener, Ramlall. Friends had already started saying their goodbyes some time ago and had given mementos, gifts; had exchanged addresses and vows of eternal friendship. Nobody had an inkling what their first posting would do to them. How different they may emerge in that 'trial by fire'. They would look the same person; but outside appearance would only belie the change within.

The corners of Ruku's suitcase were filled with so many little items: a pine flower given by Aruna, Kusum's ghazal cassette, an embroidered handkerchief from Sonal, a book from Kuldeep and Navroj's petulant looks. "I'm not giving you anything!" Words uttered with teeth clenched and eyes looking misty.

Ruku felt increasingly relaxed as the bus descended down the tarred road. What a splended day it was! From the heights she couldn't hear the hum of the valley below but the multi-coloured prospect – greens and yellows and the browns – had caught the mystery of the act of living. There was no mist anywhere, the clear blue sky proclaimed peace and happiness. The long mountain range at the distant looked obscure and impalapable as dream. Buses loaded with her friends were moving down. They had to reach Delhi by night time. The magnetism and the attractive power of Calcutta scenes, (wherein she had discovered the meaning of attachment to human beings), drew her more and more as the bus headed for the plains. Ruku was journeying towards her freedom – taking the deodar-*shirish* shaded route, feeling relaxed after a long spell of anxiety and tension.

Two memories remained that hurt her deeply. The youthful

looks of Swaruplall: an image of a young man, happily licking food off his fingers, hovered in her minds' eye. Had they abandoned him – all of them? Swarup had such hopes, he dreamt of doing so many things in life. And he died. Death snatched him away in the trivial incident of accidental drowning in the mountain stream.

And her heart palpitated when she recalled the fury of the flames that gutted the campus. The slow unstoppable march of destruction. And she had lost that miracle of symphony that Phalgun had composed – only for her. The original cassette had been placed in Ramlall's music system the night before. That music had wafted over the veranda and fallen on the dark valley like some scattered storm tossed leaves. Ramlall had kept the cassette so that he could play it for her again, the day after – fire broke that very night.

Phalgun hadn't made a copy of the cassette – the original was the only one there was – yet with what confidence he had written, "Don't bother at all, the music is dedicated to you alone. I can recreate it all over again." Could he? Would he have the inspiration – the capacity to remake, Ruku muttered to herself, gazing at the distant horizon. Tears streaming down her cheeks trickled on the *chunni*.

Phalgun exists – he can fashion such music over and over again – for her. Fire cannot touch him.

The beginning of the End.

The Mahul tree can be seen from the veranda; wood ants

crawl up and down its knotty trunk all day long. The tree seems to declare, 'I have come here to stay', through its leafy clusters, curled branches and hidden flowers and fruits. In the region where even grass shrivelled under fierce heat much care must have gone to keep a few trees alive, like the orleander, the custard apple, the *champak* and a splendid rain tree.

Gauri Nathpur – a mofussil town, though now given the status of a sub-division. Guavas were piled up and sold on the streets, rubber sandals as well. Buying and selling were conducted in the evening under hazak lamps. Rickshaws, van-rickshaw, buses all formed into a knot and stopped plying when the cowherd moved into the narrow lanes with his cows. The village comes into existence exactly at that point where the town ends. The town has no history of its own; no one knows anything about when it was built or its future.

A cradle is rocking slowly. The light inside has been put off. A bluelight is kept on, on other days. It's a full moon night and radiant moon beams have invaded the floors of the room, after bleaching the mahul tree into a milky – white colour and making the barren fields awash with light.

The cradle moves slowly because Phalgun's two arms are now the child's cradle. Phalgun loves to go about the place hugging the baby wrapped up in an old shawl. Outside, the mahul tree seems to regard them with happiness and love. The tree has a big smile. Ruku often plays records of songs or instrumental music when she is in. Phalgun prefers the quiet.

There's an interruption of the profound quiet and stillness of the surroundings if so much as a yellowed leaf falls on the ground or a fledgling sends out a cry. The smiling babe breathes imperceptibly – at times it makes only a whimpering sound in sleep. Who knows what the child thinks!

Ruku went out in a rush at five in the evening – she may be late in coming back; it could be morning. Two farm labourers were shot dead by the farmer in a village bordering the district. The village was tensed up with fear; people were agitated. The organization of the bonded labourers was gradually becoming strong in this part of the Palamao region of Bihar. The movement of the bonded labourers and the Peasant Front of the Left was gathering momentum all over the area.The farmers on their part were fortifying themselves by piling up home-made guns. The 'silence zone' between the two warring groups is now filled with gun smoke!

Ruku has to work braving all kinds of dangers. She has to be out of the house at all odd hours; at nights if necessary. Phalgun doesn't express any anxiety for her openly, merely says, "Be careful!"

They'd been here now for a year a half. Hashu was born here; has grown soft and cuddly, turned to her side and crawled. Rukmini's and Phalgun's wonder never ceases: Where did the girl come from, to fill up their entire existence?

Phalgun has a fellowship to travel in the rural areas to collect and document folk lore and folk music. He goes out with a sling bag hung on his shoulders, carrying his exercise book and cassette if the old maid servant Tamli or Ruku, herself, are at home to take care of Hashu. Though he doesn't climb mountains, he still loves to walk on the uneven roads and has got quite used to the exercise. Phalgun finds his way to all kinds of places, walking, or taking the bus and even getting on the cattle cart.

All the people in the area know him. They regard him as friend, not someone they are afraid of, or would keep a respectful distance from. Rather people who have nothing and go about barefeet and empty handed, feel secure that Phalgun has come and occupies the large house. They wave at him, slipping into the compound through the broken hedges or better still, by coming in straight through the front door. The result – a mound of complaints they have which Phalgun makes Ruku hear. The land dispute involving Tetri Munda of village Jamunia – what should be done about that, four months have already gone. What will be done about Mohin Mahato's well, Ruku? The monsoon has arrived. Ruku gets angry at times, she smiles and pulls at Phalgun's thick mop of hair. Hashu, settled comfortably in Phalgun's lap, gives Ruku's face a rub with her saliva-wet little hands. She probably feels Ruku is beating up Phalgun.

Phalgun takes up composing the symphony he lost in the fire, on the quiet afternoons when the child is asleep. It is like a game with him. Musical notes seem to appear like a row of little lambs, looking at their creator, with eyes open wide in amazement. Then Phalgun gives each and every one a special touch – one note turns into a spark of fire, another a solid piece of ice, still another a bit of dislodged meteor, a cloud ... and then? The melody floods the entire house, the rooms and the veranda and flows gushingly like the Ganges in Devprayag.

It travels to the mahul tree.The tree tries to touch the notes extending its infirm old fingers ... the shadow of that music mingles with the damp smell of flowers ... the woods of Betla are in flames on such a night in the month of *Chaitra*.

The flaming forest, the ancient mountains of the Deccan plateau, the stones – the small river keeps getting continually lost in their midst. But all nature listens to that wonderful melody – spell bound.

Glossary

Achar	pickled fruit or vegetable
Addas	get togethers
Agrahayan	winter month, roughly November
Ashar	monsoon month, roughly June-July
Ashtami	The eight day of the lunar calendar when ceremonies related to the worship of Durga goddess is on in full swing.
Asli	genuine, the "real stuff"
Atta	unhusked wheat
Azaan	call for prayer in the Mosques
Baba	Father
Bahu	Daughter-in-law
Bhadra	August
Bhaiya	Brother
Bhindi	vegetable, ladies fingers
Chaitra	March-April
Charanamrita	Holy water given by priest in the temple
Chunni	Scarf, silk or cotton
Dhoti	Loin cloth
Dida	Grandmother
Didi	Elder sister
Dure	Striped, a popular design
Gram Sevika	A village social worker
Gur	Jaggery
Jhola gur	Molasses, liquid syrup
Ma	Mother

Mashima	Maternal Aunt
Mastarmashai	Teacher, Sir, a respected form of address
Pakoras	vegetables fried in batter
Patol	a vegetable
Parathas	A kind of salty pastry
Phatua	A kind of shirt
Poush	December
Rath	The "Car festival" during the rainy season
Rotis	Indian bread prepared by hand
Sandesh	A well known children's magazine founded by Sukumar Ray and later published and edited by his son Satyajit Ray – the famous film director and writer.
Suji	Semolina